SKYLARK LOUNGE

Also by Nigel Cox

Waiting for Einstein

Dirty Work

SKYLARK LOUNGE

NIGEL COX

VICTORIA UNIVERSITY PRESS

VICTORIA UNIVERSITY PRESS
Victoria University of Wellington
PO Box 600 Wellington

© Nigel Cox 2000

ISBN 0 86473 392 5

First published 2000

ACKNOWLEDGEMENTS
'After the Gold Rush' (Neil Young), reproduced by
permission of Warner/Chappell Music Australia Pty Ltd.
Unauthorised reproduction is illegal.
'Waterloo Sunset' (Ray Davies), © 1967 Davray Music Ltd
and Carlin Music Corp. Lyrics reproduced by kind permission of
EMI Music Publishing Australia Pty Ltd.
All rights reserved.
'Bird on the Wire' (Leonard Cohen), lyrics reproduced by kind
permission of Mushroom Music Publishing/Chrysalis Music.

Printed by PrintLink, Wellington

For Susanna

Acknowledgements

I would like to acknowledge the Katherine Mansfield Memorial Trust, who awarded me the 1991 Katherine Mansfield Fellowship. This is not the novel I worked on in Menton but the time I spent there was invaluable to my development as a writer. Thanks are also due to Jo McColl, Barbara Polly and Michelle Tayler, who read the novel in draft form and made many helpful suggestions. My friends at Te Papa offered great support, in particular Kerry Jimson, Michael Keith and Diana Minchall, as did the staff of Unity Books. I am grateful to my family, who have always encouraged me. Finally I would like to thank Fergus Barrowman, Bill Manhire and Rachel Lawson at VUP for their expert editorial advice.

Paradise is with us

— Ian Wedde, 'The Story'

1

I'm going to start at the pool hall. Me behind the counter. No one in the place.

I had the morning paper. I had a CD going, one of my old reliables, everything by Ray Charles, which I can stand to listen to more or less any time. I had some decent coffee in a big white bucket of a cup that I'd picked out in Askew, thinking, yes, the day'll get off right if I have that to drink out of. I had cigars there in the box on the counter if the mood for a big smoke-up took me. The feeling was, I had things just about sorted, things back in place.

Later, as guys arrived, the mood changed. They come in with their mates, two or three in a group, and they're away from their women, away from their jobs, they have money — not that it's expensive, ten dollars or so — and the pool hall is there waiting for them, decent and clean and solid as a rock. At the counter, they talk quietly to me, because they think that's the right thing to do — me there on my stool with my paperback, the owner, the boss. No, not the boss, but the guy who is delivering this to them.

Bluesy saxophone playing softly in the background.

Every now and then I walk out among the tables, empty the ashtrays, check the toilets. Walk the aisles. Guys say, Hi, Jack, because they like saying my name — it's always a good feeling to be on a first-name basis with the proprietor. Now immediately I should say here that I'm not a big bloke. In the classic crime novels, the Raymond Chandlers and the Dashiell Hammetts, the man who has all the guys say Hi Jack to him is big, and he's easy inside his size, and nobody bothers him because he's just so big and wide that if he had to he'd pound you right down into the ground, so what's point — but that's not me. I'm just size-average, Mr Average, and in some ways that's what I think the guys enjoy, that I could just as easily be one of them, or they be me. It was important to me, then, that I appeared normal and solid. That there was no reason to be wondering about me.

On the best nights there was a terrific atmosphere in the place, with the balls clacking quietly, and the smooth green turf of the tables, each table with its rectangle of light, the lights with good soft bulbs, spreading a steady glow which made everything seem as though it'd been aged in — just short of faded, but with a history, a bit of feeling, and the racks on the walls with the cues standing evenly spaced and straight-backed in them.

Not that any of the guys who came to play there knew anything about me. They had my first name to use, Jack, like a coin they passed among themselves. But not a lot else. I was just the latest owner of the Skylark Lounge, where they'd been coming forever. As long as nothing changed about the place, no one cared who I was — which was the way I liked it.

So I had it all back under control and I had my coffee going, and old man Ray Charles going on the CD player, there was no one about yet — it was early, probably about 9.30am. I usually got the doors open about nine and then got myself set so I could enjoy the morning and get the day going right. I had the paper spread on the counter-top, working my way through to the Sports on the back page, which I always saved until last. And there on the back page was a picture which rose up at me to override all the other parts of the morning that I had so carefully put in place.

The picture was of a tennis player, Stevie Grout, being ordered from the court in an interprovincial, having punched a linesman. A dispute over a line call and Big Stevie had smacked him on the jaw. Under the headline, Out Grout!, the picture showed Stevie, head bowed, shoulders slumped, slinking away to the showers. I felt for him. I felt for the linesman too — a punch from Stevie is no laughing matter. A few months ago, Stevie punched me on the jaw — my teeth still ache.

Big Stevie used to be my son. When he was just a bub I put a tennis ball in his cot. Before he could walk even I had bought him a kiddie racquet. I taught him how to hit a topspin backhand. Now he won't speak to me. Now he won't even punch me. Now he's punching other guys instead, left, right and centre. Playing the game we both love, he throws a punch in a big match and is ejected from the court in disgrace, probably for good.

It wasn't that I'd been expecting this picture to be in the paper. I don't believe in synchronicity — as far as I'm concerned, a coincidence is a coincidence. It's important that I get this clear: I don't believe in fairies at the bottom of the garden. Because what I am going to get down in these pages will cast that into doubt.

But, looking back, it's impossible not to note how so many forces seemed at that time to be combining. Clouds were gathering. Events that should have been random seemed to be coming together to drive a wedge between me and my world.

2

At closing time, which most days was around midnight, I turned on the main fans so they'd suck the smoke out, turned off the lights over the green tables, and started locking the locks. Then, walking from upper Cuba Street to the car park through the dark, I never felt any fear. Wellington isn't that kind of city. I know a gay bloke who disagrees, and I guess I might feel different if I wore a skirt, but for me it's hard to avoid the feeling that most of the time common sense rules, and select committees, and citizens and ratepayers. Wellington just isn't a big-drama kind of town.

I lived in a fringe of the city, down Happy Valley Road, in a bit of a rumpty palace of a house banged together by some DIY no-hoper. It was cheap and had a section and we had three kids and, at the time we bought, not a lot of options. Plus there was a nice feeling to the place, or Shelley would never have even glanced at it. It had a drive which angled steeply from the road, and a parking pad which was a challenge to manoeuvre into if you were coming home late after a good time, and then it was just five short steps before you were closing the back door and shutting the world out.

Gotta be able to shut that world out.

But the time I'm trying to make myself focus on here wasn't a night-time; it was in the morning, 8.15-ish — back about eighteen months before Big Stevie's final meltdown. I was in my car, headed up Happy Valley Road. It was a big car, old, a 1965 Wolseley 6/110 Mk II, pale green, and I was set deep in the leather driver's seat with my arms out straight and my hands sort of bolted to the giant steering wheel, as though

I was engaged in a life-or-death struggle for control of the Wolseley-monster. I probably looked like a bit of a wanker in that car — when I was in it I took myself pretty seriously. Well, it's like driving a living room around, it's so big, and inside it you feel like nothing can touch you.

So I'm on Happy Valley Road, in my big car, in the morning, and then I start to notice the weather. It seems to be closing in. At first it's just some low cloud, and then next time I look the cloud seems really solid, and sort of metallic, and spread thickly across the entire sky in an impenetrable layer.

I glance up ahead and I can see a fair way — along the dark surface of the road to the brow of the hill and then on beyond that to a distant strip of blue between the hilltop and the underside of the cloud. The blue is shining, there's a brightness of some sort in it. And the brightness seems to be coming towards me. Now I see that in fact the brightness is part of the cloud, it appears that the lower edge of the cloud, the far edge, is shining, and that it's coming towards me — and that the reason it's coming towards me is because the cloud layer is tilting. Yes, dammit, the whole cloud layer is tilting to meet the ground, forming an angle, a wedge, which I'm driving into.

I slow the car.

Immediately some bloke behind me honks, swerves round, then charges on towards Brooklyn. Well, he didn't have any problem, so I speed up again. But the sense that I'm driving myself into a crash is too strong and I have to take my foot off. The cloud is right there in front of me now. It hasn't tilted so far as to be vertical; it's making an angle with the road and the vee of that angle has come steadily on to be right in front of me, an immense wall of shifting grey. It isn't vague, like fog.

It has a definite, compact look to it, solid — and solid is what it proves to be, because as I drive slowly forward my car gets jammed in the angle between the cloud and the road.

I twist to check the rear window — blue skies back there. So I go to shift into reverse. It's then that I realise that I'm still in drive. When I listen I can hear the engine. But we're not going anywhere! I sit for a moment, thinking, I'm wrecking this car. Then I open my door and peer out at the tyres. No smoke. No burning rubber. But they're still turning! It's like an illusion — it just doesn't make sense. I'm still on the ground, there's no gap between tyre and road. The tyres are just spinning happily away.

I feel deeply confused.

Then it occurs to me that I'm in danger. I'm right in the middle of the road. One car has passed me and any moment another is going to come roaring up from behind and hit me. I can't get the Wolseley to go anywhere, so I put it into park, slide across to the passenger's door, and get out.

I'm stooped low. Now that I no longer have the roof of the car as a buffer, the cloud ceiling is threateningly close and I don't want to touch it. Beside the road is a footpath and the footpath is made of asphalt. Good. In this moment mundane details are important to me. In the cracks of the asphalt lichen is glowing, an intense yellow — is that normal? Then there's a little grassy verge, and a five-wire fence, and, from the other side of the fence, a goat is watching me. Ogling me with its alien eye. Then it goes back to eating the grass. As I'm watching it I'm thinking, that goat's okay — animals always know if something weird is happening. Then I hear a car coming, it's coming up the road, fast, and immediately I know it's going to drive straight into the back of the Wolseley. Interestingly, even under the pressure of that moment, I don't stand up —

I really don't want to touch that sky. I watch as the car comes on, you know how you judge road speed and what will happen — he's got to swerve *now*, I'm thinking, and I wince and shy away. But there's no smash.

The next car does exactly the same — just keeps on coming. Drives right on. *Through* the Wolseley.

I sit on the verge, breathing through my mouth. The goat is kneeling now, at the end of its chain, straining, neck twisted, to reach those blades of grass at the very rim of its eating circle. I've always hated goats, their devil eyes, and in this moment I particularly hate this one. I can smell it, like greasy wool, and I can hear the ripping sound it makes as it tears the grass with its teeth. Stained teeth. Goat breath. I'm over-whelmed by a feeling of revulsion — I'm sick to my stomach.

I make myself look up into the cloud.

I'm crouched low beside the fence. The sky is right there, at arm's length — a murky, swirling surface, moving slowly like the sludge in a river eddy. Behind the sludge there appears to be a solid grey layer that extends in every direction like a low roof. Slowly, I extend a hand. The surface swirl seems to find a focus — as my fingertips get closer a whirlpool begins to form in the cloud, right at the point where they're about to touch. When I draw my hand back the movement dies.

I have another go. I'm watching my fingers as though I might never see them again. I touch. The surface sludge is like dry water — something seems to run across my fingertips, like sand, but it has no substance. I rub my fingertips together. It occurs to me that my fingerprints are being taken — that I'm making an impression of some sort. In the ceiling of cloud there is now a great slow circle of movement with my fingers at its centre.

Another car goes past.

My hand goes higher. But there's nothing more to feel — just the sense that a current, cool and dry, is slipping round it. Or perhaps that it's slipping into something that is taking its shape, a sort of mould. But no sense of constriction. I also have the sensation of being on camera, that I'm being watched, that I'm performing. That damned goat won't take its eyes off me. It's appealing to me — 'What?' I say, irritated. I pull my hand back and the fingers come away quite freely. Is there a sense of slipping out of contact? The way a man slips out of a woman, that regretted withdrawal. I stare at my palm, at the pink blotchiness of it. No change. One, two, three, four, four fingers and the hitchhiker's thumb. Staring at your hand, it's kind of an idiot thing to do. There's nothing to learn there. So I straighten up.

As my head goes through the cloud there is a pop in my ears, and then the cloud disappears.

On a beautiful blue-sky day I am standing beside Happy Valley Road in the company of a goat. Completely alone. The sense that I have been separated from my family, from anyone that loves me, or even knows me, is overwhelming. A car goes past, horn howling, and I see that the Wolseley is sitting right in the middle of the left lane, a real danger. I run to get it out of the way. Its engine is still going — when I release the handbrake, off we go. I drive slowly, frowning up through the windscreen at the clear blue sky.

3

Okay. What I have to say here is that I have a stable mental history. And because of that I find it hard writing this stuff down. That's reasonable, surely. I mean, I'm just not a paranormal kind of guy.

And then this thing happened to me.

Right, you're a lawyer and you live in Wadestown, and one morning you look out the window and a lion is savaging your dachshund. Impossible! But it's not impossible. It's *unlikely*. Think of all the things that happen on the news. No matter how weird, they always turn out to have been possible. But what happened to me on Happy Valley Road just was not possible.

So, on the morning that I'm trying to describe, my sense of the right order of things just abandoned me. I felt I was driving the Wolseley through the air, and couldn't be sure that I wasn't. My scalp felt as though it had been scratched — on the inside. Trees were bending in to look, the road ahead was flexing and buckling.

By crawling along the curb, I got to the brow of the climb, through the hilltop village, and got started on the long run down the Brooklyn hill on the other side. I caught sight of the city below. It looked remote, closed to me. And I felt that, in my condition, that was only reasonable — I wasn't fit to take my place there. But where to run to? Then, on the left, the Renouf Tennis Centre appeared. Tennis, it's always been a kind of home base for me, and quickly I turned in, parked, and went inside to just sit in the stands, from where I could watch some guys hit some balls.

The Renouf Centre has fourteen courts laid out like an estate, like a vineyard, where you can go and indulge your tennis obsession among the like-minded. I have always loved that company. That sound, echoing off the hills, of the ball being definitively hit — thock! The little gasp when the canister of balls is opened and the vacuum is broken — it's like something taking its first breath. And the balls themselves waiting in there, glowing fluorescent eggs, just eager to bounce. The squeaking of the shoes, and the sweating, the swearing, and the speaking of the score. Fifteen love, thirty fifteen, thirty forty, deuce — it's such a mantra. Game, set and match. The scoring system in tennis is a frame you can live within. There's such certainty there, such logical progression. It's the same with the court. Those beautiful white lines, the fat confidence of them. The regularity. Every court the same, with the lines the same distance apart, the earth measured into identical plots all over the planet. And within that scoring system, within those lines, such possibility! No game is ever the same. The truth is, I am at home in tennis. I am happy in it. That morning I stayed in the Renouf Centre for three and a half hours. I dredged up highlights from my life in the game — once I was coached by Rod Laver! My serve with the evil kick! Playing with Stevie, the first time he beat me — I was so happy. Then I realised they thought I might be trying to look up the skirts of the teenage girls in the coaching squad — I saw I was going to be approached, and left.

I made myself go outside and get into the Wolseley again. I put it in drive. I got on the highway and let it carry me out to Pukerua Bay.

We'd come often to Pukerua when I was a kid. Great hook of bay. Immense eyeball of ocean, with seabirds flying long lines across it. Blue-green island long on the horizon, looking like Te Rauparaha's mere that I saw in Te Papa. In the foreground, the rock pools where we poddled, shrimping with milk bottles, prising limpets. For years, we went there every holidays. And then we stopped coming.

Something happened.

We used to come to a bach along the beach road that belonged to Mum and Dad's friends, the Clinghorns. Flagons on the veranda. Fry-ups for brekkie. Me and the Clinghorn kids playing the wide game all over the scrambly hillsides. One morning we'd taken the steep track up to the tennis courts near Muri Station. It's strange playing in those old outdoor courts; you're in a frame of rusted wire, a sort of cage. The wind rattled the flax bushes. The white tramlines on the asphalt were mostly chipped off. All around, the hills stood, humpbacked green lumps, and then there was the sky — the court was on the top of a lump, you seemed to be playing up in the air. The game began. Then, I remember, I started watching the clouds go past. I just couldn't stop looking at them. I was about eight or nine. I sat down on the court — I sat down on the court in the middle of a game, and started staring up, past the clouds, into the blue depths of the skies. It pissed the Clinghorns off.

Parking the Wolseley now at the far end of the beach road, in the turning area and picnic spot that wasn't there in the old days, I started walking back towards the baches. There was a dirty wind blowing grit into my face. The sea heaved on my left; on my right the hillside rose steeply, covered in springy bushes and flax, divided by rock slides that came down like rivers. The flax rattled, an old sound. I could hear it, hear it — the sea was noisy, I strained to listen.

I remembered that I'd sat on the tennis court and looked

up into the sky. Nine years old. I was trying to find something. The flax rattled like my brains. I'd told Mum and Dad about what had happened to me and they got pissed off too. They started looking at me sideways. Watching back.

I came along past the last couple of baches — there was the Clinghorns', third from the end. I kept my head down, in case anyone living there might know me. It'd been nearly forty years. I hadn't seen any of the Clinghorn kids for, oh, yonks.

It was along here.

I went past the old boatshed, hidden now in the shoreline scrub, and on, across the little bridge. I was still going along the road, but that wasn't it.

It was down on the beach.

A track through the scrub appeared on my left and I took it, through the overgrowth, flax and taupeta scrub that stood waist-deep above the high-water mark. Bloody flax bushes. I've always hated that rattle, gets on my nerves. I couldn't look up. I knew that if I did I'd see that the sky was made of metal, that it was tilting down to make an angled trap for me. I was really starting to remember now. I came out onto the shingle beach and trudged along above the seaweed and wrack. Gulls screamed at me. The wind was annoying, it kept making me want to turn back. My legs were heavy. I knew exactly where I had to go — not far now.

4

I'd already survived one bout of remembering.

This was back in the early 1970s when *After the Gold Rush* came out. That's so long ago now, I guess I should say, when the Canadian folk-rock singer Neil Young released a record album (vinyl) of that name. The record was a huge hit and you heard it at every suburban hippy party, in every supermarket. I used to sing bits of it as I strode around town in my fringed Buffalo Bill jacket and the jeans with many-coloured patches. 'Only Love Can Break Your Heart', 'Don't Let It Bring You Down', 'Oh, Lonesome Me' — it made you feel good that Neil felt so bad. Brilliant record. But there were words in its title song that I really hated. I'd find myself singing this song and start to grind my teeth. Neil wrote this about me — sometimes I caught myself thinking that. Starting to hyperventilate now . . .

> *All in a dream, all in a dream,*
> *the loading had begun,*
> *flyin' Mother Nature's*
> *silver seed*
> *to a new home in the sun.*
>
> *Well, I dreamed I saw the silver spaceships flyin'*
> *in the yellow haze of the sun.*
> *There were children cryin'*
> *and colours flyin'*
> *all around the chosen ones.*

That was me, I was a chosen one. Well, it's not hard to think that when you're nineteen, which I was in 1970. Except that I was a nerd who couldn't relate, a streak of weasel-piss, a bedroom obsessive, goggle-eyed geek freak who could instantly produce a two-hour monologue on any given Dylan lyric. I guess I don't have to say, yet, who Bob Dylan is. Sensible people avoided me, I know they did, I could feel it, and I didn't blame them. I wanted to avoid me — I spent the whole time imagining I was someone else. Wasted years! And the music of that time, it colluded in this wastage. It told you you were nowhere and that there was a perfect world waiting, but . . . elsewhere.

Except for that song of Neil Young's. That song was so to the point, it scared me. If anyone ever found out what that song made me remember, I was wearing the fruitcake label for life.

I mean, I imagine you've gathered by now what I'm talking about. I've hinted around enough, I've been preparing you. It's going to be an anticlimax now, you're going to say, yeah, absolutely, Jack, you're going to tell us you were abducted by aliens.

And I am. I'm going to make myself say that.

Let me state something here. Apart from the sun, the nearest star to the Earth is Alpha Centauri. Its galaxy is the nearest place that an alien species could live. For aliens from there to be on Earth today, even if they had a spacecraft that could travel a million miles an hour, they would have had to have left home in the time of Moses. I do know that. What I'm about to tell you, well . . . I already said it. It's impossible.

Okay, let's get it over with: when I was I kid we went out to Pukerua Bay. We always stayed at the Clinghorns' bach. I slept in a sleep-out, in a bunk. I was about nine. And during the night I started to experience being abducted by aliens.

Even though it was dark, in the experience the world would be brightly lit and I would go down to the beach and stand blinking on the shingle. I would be alone. I would go stumbling along as though I was in a dream, and keep going until I came to the right spot. I could tell it was the right spot because everything in the universe was pulling me towards it — like it was the centre of gravity. It was as though I was being led by my stomach, and as soon as I arrived my ears would go pop. As though I'd passed through something. As though I was now locked in. I'd blink. I don't really know what state I was in. Suddenly I'd seem to be wide awake and on the beach and looking out over the water. I say looking but I couldn't see anything much, because all I was interested in was the island, Kapiti, glowing there on the horizon, and I'd stare and stare as though I was completely fascinated by it. The weather would be clear and still, the air would always be so sweet that you wanted to drink it. I always felt terrific — and then the gravity would shift, and that right place to be would move so that it was ahead of me again, out in the water, towards the island. So off I'd go. On the water there'd be this silvery stuff, light, moving on the surface. It made a narrow strip, like the path the moon makes on water, that stretched out towards the island, and I was on it. Not stumbling now — I knew exactly where I was going. That air would just be making me sing!

I don't really know if I walked or ran or if I flew along that silvery stuff. I'd set off towards the island and then I seemed to pick up speed. As I did I'd feel myself starting to rise, the silver strip would bend in the air, rising up as though it was alive. It wasn't very wide but I never felt I was going to fall off it. Once I remember glancing down and I could see the ocean far below on either side of me. It was really clear, I could see all the fish in it, and I knew what kind of fish they were. I should explain that. I could see the multitude of ocean creatures, really clearly, more and more clearly the longer I concentrated on them. That's a wandering sea-anemone. That's a sea urchin. That's a school of pipe fish. I knew their names, and everything about them. That's a John Dory, and that mark on its side is supposed to be Jesus's thumbprint. Jesus was this man who . . . It was wonderful to be so knowledgeable, to know our world as well as that — as though, against all odds, I'd remembered everything I'd ever been told. I felt like a genius. And the world itself was wonderful too — the astonishing diversity of it, and all of it so busy and alive. Even the dead bits like the rocks — they seemed to be sort of humming. As I went higher I could see the coast curving away to the north, and then the outline of the southern end of the island, and then finally I could see the whole North Island, that shape we all know from maps, I could see it down there under me. It was extraordinary to be flying — I can't tell you. Just air, everywhere. Air under your tummy. Coming through your clothes. Cold air on your cheeks, in your mouth. Sweet, sweet air. And your body rising through it, charmed and complete. I can't tell you how much I loved the North Island. The shape of it.

I never felt scared.

I'd go higher and higher, up towards the stars, and then my ears would pop again. And I'd give a little shiver. As I came out of the shiver I would recognise that something had happened to me, but I wasn't sure what. I'd feel at a loss for a moment. Then I'd blink again, and look around at where I'd arrived.

★

Everybody always wants to know what it is like inside the spaceship. Remember when they advertised the special extended version of *Close Encounters of the Third Kind* — they said, 'We go *inside*.'

I have seen *Close Encounters*. It was pretty dumb. But in general I try to avoid things on SETI, the dreck books, the Amazing Stories-type TV programmes — those blurry pictures of hubcaps and flying cigars. It's such wishful thinking. The Kaikoura UFOs — what wank fluid. People are just dying for there to be *more*. For there to be fairies, or God, or life after death, or hobbits, or Heaven, or Superman, or angels, or ghosts — anything that lets them believe that there's more than *this*. Give us magic! And if they can't have magic then they want toys. Technology. Machines that make it seem like there's magic. That's why everyone wants to know what it's like inside, I reckon, because secretly they know there's no magic, we don't really believe in magic any more, not unless we're soft, but we do hang onto the hope that machines will be able to do magic things — and that the things they do will be real. And we think that spacecraft will have magic machines inside. So — what is it like inside? That's what everyone wants to know.

But they were really careful about that, the aliens. They wouldn't let me see. I just hung there in the air, way up above the world. I was inside something. I was in the spacecraft. But I didn't even have a seat. I could *feel* the ship around me, but there was nothing to see.

When I thought about it afterwards — just after I'd stopped straining to think about it — the image that came to my mind was that I'd been in a silvery room about the size of a squash court. A kind of lounge, maybe.

I had lots of images. I didn't have to think about what had

happened, or strain to remember. I knew exactly what'd happened to me. I was nine years old — mind unfucked-up by drugs or craziness. All I wanted to do in life was hit tennis balls.

When I picture what happened to me while I was in the ship, I see myself turning somersaults in the air. Slowly. Head over heels. Round and round like a wheel. Weightless. Frictionless. Going nowhere — a mote turning in space. At the same time I was incredibly still. I had to be still so that I could see with such perfect focus. I looked down and I could see everything that I knew about. It was the most wonderful sensation, to see my home as if for the first time. Everything familiar, and yet looking so fantastic, as though it had just been washed by a big rain or something, so that you just wanted to give an in-depth explanation of whatever your eye fell on. My school. The street. Our house. My mum and dad, sleeping in bed. My sisters. When I thought about it later, this was strange — because they weren't really at home in bed, they were out at Pukerua Bay, in the bach. But it didn't surprise me that they were home. Nothing surprised me. I knew about everything that I looked at. I recognised everything.

I could see down into the grass. There was a hay paddock over the fence from our house and I could see right down between the stalks of the hay. I could see mice down in there, and beetles, and little ants. I could see the joints of the ants' bodies. They were so brilliantly put together. The hairs on the back of the mouse — his coat was so fine. He was quivering in the world he lived in, down among the roots of the haystalks. And down between the hairs on his back, the mites that lived on him. The tiny translucent bodies of the mites. The organs in there, the loops of the digestive system. I knew about all of this. It was the most pleasurable sensation I'd ever felt, to see everything in my home-world and know it for what it was.

And that was just the natural world. The natural world seems to have been perfectly designed — never mind by whom. I'm all for the theory of evolution, but that's not what I saw when I looked at the mice. They seemed finished, perfect. It was in the world where I lived, the human world, that I could see evolution. The pale yellow cup sitting on the formica of the kitchen bench — the handle of the cup. That handle had evolved so that it was exactly right for two fingers to go through. As I stared at the cup its design was apparent. Its cleverness. Human cleverness was revealed to me. The forks. The spoons. The knives. The way they lay side by side in their plastic trays, elegant and well ordered and just made so perfectly for their intended use. The formidable nature of the taps, positioned so intelligently over the sink, where they held back the water, releasing it in controlled quantities. The catches on the cupboard doors. The hinges. The knobs on the Shacklock with their circle of calibrations. And the way the light fell on all this — the window, placed there in the wall of the room so that light could enter and surround everything. So clever to put the window just there. So clever to divide the rooms of the house like that, with a room for every purpose. And the things that didn't work — the pantry overfilled so that its door wouldn't shut, the fancy paperknife, the ugly jug up on the high shelf that was never used — these things filled me with such tender feelings. I wanted to defend them, to explain them. But they stood there, apparent, naked. They needed so badly — it does seem that these inanimate things needed — to be part of the whole.

There wasn't any music or anything.

The way the houses sat on their sections, each section with paths and gardens in squares and fences. The way the sections were next to each other, in streets, which were connected by roads, and intersections, and stop signs, and street lights, and bridges, and car parks. Seeing all this — the way the streets connected to make towns, and the way the towns gave us a purchase on the land. The way we'd designed our world.

Then that would be it. I'd have a thought that amounted to, 'So that's the way it is.' And I would know that it was over, and that I was about to start going back.

Going back was slow. It was like a slide — I would be up there in the air, then only part of me would be, and another part would be sliding back down to earth. Like a droplet going down a fence-wire. It was the most thrilling sensation, to be long, stretched from air to earth. Then I'd be back on the beach with the sea breeze in my face, blinking.

With a smile on my face.

The other thing people always want to know, of course, is, what do they look like? How many eyes, how many legs? But the aliens never showed themselves to me. I never knew where they were from or what they were doing or why they'd chosen me.

So how did I know I was abducted by aliens? (Abducted? But it's what you always say.) Since I never had any evidence of them. Well — I just knew. I had no proof whatsoever. I was abducted by aliens. I don't expect anyone to believe me. I'm just saying what happened.

I did hear their voices. Or, voice — just as I was starting to slide back a voice would say to me, 'We are grateful to you, Jack Grout.'

The words formed inside my head. They came up there, like words coming up on a big electronic scoreboard at the cricket — I could see them. They were blue, a cold blue, and furred round the edges, where they faded back to white. They formed slowly — furred blue words lodged deep within a slab of ice. *We are grateful to you.* At the same time I'd start to hear them in my head. They formed slowly there too, from a bank of sound. The sound would come towards me, like a flight of aircraft, and the words would emerge out of that sound. *We. Are. Grateful. To. You.* (Aliens always have the same trouble with full-stops as John Banks.) I wouldn't figure out for sure what was being said until they were nearly past — until the meaning assembled itself. The voice sounded . . . alien! I mean, I couldn't listen to it and go, oh, well, that's a man, and he's old, and he's been well educated — the way that we do. I couldn't find a person in that voice. It was a machine voice, and my idea was that it didn't come from the mouth of an alien — they'd dreamed up a machine to speak to me.

That was what I thought, then.

Afterwards, as I said, I'd be back on the beach. I'd be looking up into the sky and just getting a fix on where I was, when a strange thing began to happen to the sea breeze. It would start to blow the daylight away. It'd get darker and darker and then when it was completely dark, suddenly I'd wake up — and I'd be in a bunk in the Clinghorns' bach, in the sleep-out, and instead of day it'd be night, and instead of being in company I'd be alone. I was nine years old.

So there I was again on that same beach, only now I was forty-seven. Cold breeze in my teeth. The island still out there. The rattle of flax. Gravel crunching when I moved my feet. Stink of old seaweed. Gulls. Stink of the sea. The sea grey and heaving like my thoughts.

5

When I was nine I survived because I was just a kid. Mum and Dad were worried that I was losing my marbles, but everyone accepts that kids go through weird phases — they hoped that's what I was doing and plugged on.

I started getting distracted. That time on the tennis court with the Clinghorn kids — staring at the sky. Tuning out. Wondering. I mean, when you're a kid you try and figure things out. You think things — standing in the back yard, looking up, thinking, Why can't I see right out into space? Does the beam that comes out of my eye get tired and just stop, or what? You don't talk things over, in case you're dumb and everybody else has figured it all out ages ago. You just get on with reloading your machine gun or whatever the game is. But inside your head . . . I started tuning out at school. Which was unusual for me — I liked school. We had some great teachers, I can still remember their names, Miss Walters, Miss Curle, Mr Parkin, and I enjoyed the chanting: seven sixes are forty-two, seven sevens are forty-nine. I've never been an adventurous person. I like to know what's expected of me so I can get on and do it. Just tell me what you want. So when they began to say — Mum and Dad, the teachers — What's on your mind, Jack? I told them. Whenever we go out to Pukerua Bay, the aliens take me up in their spacecraft. *Yes, right*. And when I'm up there I can see everything. *Go on*. And I can understand everything. And I explain it all to them. And then they say they're grateful to me, and then I slide back down to the beach, and then I'm back in bed. *Good, thank you, Jack, that's very good*.

They got me a psychologist — that was pretty special back in those days — and sat me in a comfortable chair in his clinic and made me say it all over again. Then he explained to them what was happening, so that I could hear, and then explained it all again to me. 'Recurrent dream motif' — I remember that phrase — turned into, 'You've been having a special kind of dream, Jack.' And they made me tell it all again, but this time they made me keep saying, in the dream. 'In my dream, what happened next was . . .' 'That's a *very* interesting dream, Jack.'

Then they put me in another school. They told me I shouldn't tell anyone about my dream, or think about it, or have it again if I could help it. They got me a tennis coach, which I'd been bugging them about for ages, and they made sure I got plenty of exercise and went to bed tired. Run down to the shop, will you, Jacky-boy, and get me some pipe cleaners. I didn't mind. I didn't mind any of it. They were my mum and dad, they were just trying to do their best. I could see they were worried about me. I didn't want them looking at me all the time, monitoring me. We'd always been allowed to run pretty free. Ours was the last house in a street where the streets ran out — over the fence there was a hay paddock, and then there were pine trees. My friends and I used to disappear out the back for hours and come home covered in mud. As long as your clothes weren't ripped it wasn't a problem.

So I stopped telling anyone about the aliens. I saw that it'd been a near thing, that I'd nearly become a weirdo, a kid that the other kids called names. I got good at doing what everyone else was doing again, I studied up on doing the right thing.

But I kept a little cube in my head for the aliens to live in. I kept them inside there and never let them get out. I kept them alive. I fed them explanations, pointed things out to them.

My parents stopped taking us to Pukerua Bay. They bought a bach of their own, at Ocean Beach, and on our holidays we always went there.

After that, the aliens contacted me once more. It was the only time they ever took me when I was sleeping in my own bed at home. Everything was the same — except when it was time for the encounter to end. At the end they said, 'We. Will. Always. Be. Grateful. To. You. Jack. Grout.' At the time I didn't realise it, but this was a goodbye. They never came for me again.

They lived on in the cube in my head but as time went by I didn't visit the cube so often. Months went by when I didn't think about them. Just every now and then. Then years. As I said earlier, I had a little crisis when that Neil Young song was released, and suddenly I couldn't get the aliens out of my mind. Then I got another girlfriend and that passed.

I walked slowly along the beach at Pukerua Bay, staring down at the stones. My shoes crunched. My hair was tugged all about by the wind. I had never at any time in my life believed that what had happened to me was only a dream. But I'd managed to stop thinking about it — for, what, thirty-odd years. Got married, got married again, had three kids. Got a life. Now the aliens were coming back. I didn't think I could face it.

I considered admitting myself. Porirua was just up the motorway. But that would have been stupid. I knew I wasn't deranged. I had to keep the aliens quiet, that was all.

6

I got stuck in at work. This was back before I owned the pool hall. At that time I was Advertising Services Manager for Wellington's everlasting morning paper, the *Dominion*, where I'd put in nine uninspiring years. There's nothing like the news industry to reduce your day to fish 'n' chip wrapping. You never work towards anything, except your next deadline. It was a kind of oblivion and I hate to say this but I loved it. It was so mindless. I turned up, I made sure that we had the material we needed to print the ads that the ad sales department had sold, I got on the blower for someone to get us the material if we didn't. Everything changed when we went online — for instance, all the people who said 'the blower' retired — then the place settled down again and we went back to looking out for the next deadline, again.

Day after day.

What I loved was the people. I'd never worked anywhere where so many other humans were around you all day. You knew their names, you heard them say their pet phrases, you saw them wear their clothes. You saw their little ways. This one giving up smoking again. This dreamy one falling in love with that unpleasant one. This serious one puzzling away at what to do with her life. I would go home and tell Shelley all about it, like it was a mini-series.

But it wasn't the kind of job you could do much with. When I say I got stuck in, well . . . I organised a coat of paint for the dovecotes where we kept the film we had lined up for the next couple of days. I redesigned the form where we recorded the material that we'd cleared. I went to work on

Ian J, this kid I had working for me who had too many brains, and got him to go back to university — he was talking up a revolution among my troops. I tidied, and planned, and made charts, and schedules, and timetables . . .

I bought four new ties and after I'd been wearing them for three weeks solid I went to see the big man about a promotion. From behind his belly he intoned: We've got our eye on you, Jack. You're doing a great job. The newspaper is built on people like you. You have a really solid future here. Of course, at this particular time, Jack. A man like you would realise. I don't think we have to spell it out to a man like you. Jack. No, he didn't. So I went straight out of there and downtown and I bought the pool hall.

It actually happened like that, all in a huge confused rush.

I'd been playing there on and off for years — me and my old schoolmate Fatty, or the guys from the tennis club. Suddenly everything came together. The aliens stopped my car, I got a fifteen hundred dollar tax refund, I bought four new ties, the pool hall was for sale, I looked at the big man and saw I was going to turn into him. I was forty-seven. Suddenly I went downtown and rearranged our mortgage, borrowed some capital from Fatty, and bought that pool hall, and then I went home and told Shelley.

Within a year she'd moved the kids out.

But I'm getting ahead of myself. Okay — to summarise: the aliens abducted me when I was nine. I kept them in a cube inside my head. I took care never to let them out. I watched my thoughts and made sure that no one knew that I believed in UFOs.

Years passed.

And then they stopped my car.

I'd always known what would happen if ever I slept in any bed that wasn't my own. Now that they'd made contact again, next time I was available to them it was odds on that they would take me up for a session. I do know how dumb that sounds. It sounds like some white trash truckdriver from a southern state, who is swearing to god in a crap documentary — 'The lil' green men, they come an' take me.' But it was what I was stuck inside. I knew what was going to happen. It was like suddenly realising that the underdogs were going to beat the champions this weekend — you just know. No, it was stronger than that. It was a certainty that was an integral part of every cell of me. This knowledge was who I was. I had no doubt whatsoever: they were coming for me.

I tried to act normal. But then I'd just quit my job and bought the pool hall, that wasn't normal, and so a new era began and no matter how hard I tried I just couldn't get things to proceed.

For a start, with Shelley. When I told her we now owned a pool hall and that our mortgage had just gone up, she just went on painting. We were in Stevie's room, which was an add-on at the back of the garage, and she was making it nice for him, not that he wanted her to, Stevie liked it grungy, but Shelley knew better and was bringing a woman's touch to his fucked-up adolescence. Chalky white walls, with a picture she'd bought, a real artwork by this guy you might have heard of, Michael Shepherd, weird, done with coloured pencils, a pale drawing of paper stars standing on the tips of sewing needles which were stuck into cotton reels — as I say, weird, but it sort of made you think of a fragile Christmas or the tiny magic of an embroiderer's casket or something. She paid $1,200 for it (see, she bought things without asking too) and then hung it in his room, and now she was painting the sills a sandy terracotta colour to go with it. And she paused and, making sure that her brush was over the drip-cloth so the carpet wouldn't get spotted, turned to look at me.

'A pool hall?'

I nodded. I was finding this hard. She nodded back. Then she went on painting. I sat on the end of Stevie's bed, watching. I love to watch her do things. You're not allowed, are you, just to watch. People get unnerved. When I'm playing tennis it always spooks me if I think anyone might see how I'm playing a shot. But people are so good to look at. Shelley was kneeling, she had her hair back behind her ears, she was holding the brush so steady and she was making a straight line of colour where the sill met the wall. Tongue between her teeth. The light from the window catching the side of her cheek, so that her freckles were highlighted. Go ahead and join up the dots, she used to say to me.

I waited for her to stop again, but she just kept on dipping and brushing, getting that colour on. 'Shell?' I had to say.

'Go on, tell me,' she said.

But she wouldn't stop working. So I had to tell her back. I got angry with her. Everything I said sounded really plausible. Everything I said sounded like bullshit. I was really angry that she was making me do it this way — suddenly I wrapped it all up by saying, 'Anyway, I guess we can always sell it. I mean, there must be more than one idiot out there.'

She laughed.

Later in the day I caught her looking at me. 'What?' I said.

I had to chase her to make her tell me. She turned around halfway up the stairs and gazed down. 'That job was pretty shitty, wasn't it,' she said. 'I don't blame you.' And she pushed me away and went on up the stairs.

But she did. Blame me. She found me wanting. She thought me over and there'd been a pattern. This was what she said, later. I'd been going off on my own, she said.

That was such a strange thing to say, when I knew that I'd been making such a bird of sleeping in my own bed.

And then I was trying to be the efficient proprietor of a small business. I bought the pool hall on not much more than a whim and now I had to make it work — it had to provide half our income. For the first month we were eating our savings.

But that changed. In fact I got the pool hall figured pretty smartly. A coat of paint. The right hours, the right music. How to talk to the guys. Who to discourage, who to give free games to. Who always got the best table, no matter what. But I just couldn't escape what was coming to me.

Normally a project like that would just swallow my life. I love to throw myself at things. Normally my entire person would be consumed. And I was consumed. But not entirely, that's all. There was a cube in my head.

And when finally the cube decided to expand, there was no way I could stop it.

The real trouble started with a break-in down at the pool hall. The phone went at 2.30 in the morning, the police calling to say, You better come down here. There was no damage, nothing of significance taken, a few packets of cigars — some boys just had to have a game, probably — but the locks were busted. No problem, officer — I'll just sit her for what's left of the night.

I pulled my stool into a corner behind the counter, leaned my back against the wall, put my feet up, and got set to listen to a best-of CD. Dusty Springfield's *Greatest Hits* looked good.

Sitting there at one end of the long shadowy rectangle of the pool hall, to the sound of 'Wishin' and Hopin'', I drifted into the night. 'Goin' Back' put me into a kind of swoon. By the time I was two bars into 'Island of Dreams' I was slipping my moorings.

My eyelids weighed a ton. My head snapped back and forth on the hinge of my neck. All around, the pool hall swam, green tables floating like islands in the half-dark. Dusty's voice came into me like a drug.

It never occurred to me . . .

As I went under I had no fear.

7

On my stool there behind the counter, the music seemed never to end. Well, I did have the CD player on repeat. 'Son of a Preacher Man' went past about eight times. And the pool hall seemed to have no ending either. It stretched on, table after table, out into the night. Weird. Then gravity began to release its hold. Things started to drift. Up, up went the pool hall, turning, whirling gracefully, a hawk in an updraft. The door, without its lock, had swung open — the moon kept sliding past the doorway as though it was orbiting me.

As we turned, by the swinging light of the moon I could see that the pool tables had risen from the floor and were floating. One of the tables had a set of balls on it that hadn't been cleared away and they were floating too. They hung in the air like the dots inside a column of DNA, seeming to turn slowly inside the hall along with the tables and the cubes of chalk. Occasionally a ball would bump and there would be that pleasant click of billiard balls in contact — as though a game was being played in three dimensions. I found this a bemusing thought. Drunk-making. Silly. I felt a bit silly, and not unhappy. I lifted myself from my chair and stepped out from behind the counter. Or tried to step — my legs weighed nothing and in fact seemed not to be there at all. When I let go of the counter I began to rise.

I floated out into the room, tumbling slowly.

I was afraid of the doors. They were open and I was scared that if I went near them I might be sucked out into the sky and float off among the stars. When finally I drifted past one of the tables I gave myself a good shove off it and headed back towards the far end of the hall.

I caught a ball. I plucked it from the air and together we floated. The tables went on forever, like a hall of mirrors. I could still see the counter and, when I listened, hear Dusty's voice, faint, like a tinny radio, far away.

I was still holding the ball when I realised I was feeling weight return to my limbs. It was a death feeling, like that heaviness that comes sucking down if you lie in the bath while the water drains out. The tables were drifting back to their places. The hall was spinning slower.

I came to rest amid the tables.

Nothing. Silence.

I waited. Out the doorway there were stars — I seemed to be looking at them side-on, and I wondered how far I'd journeyed. Then I had the impulse to go across to the door and look out. So as not to lose control, I crawled. The night air was cool and very fresh. Looking down, I saw the blue marble of our planet, deep in space below me. Earth's moon, a withered yellow pea, proceeding around its orbit. The stars, long spears of light.

Where was I?

I imagined myself falling, all the way down to Earth — suddenly dizzy, I crawled backwards and stood, carefully grasping a table. But then even the table wasn't to be relied on. Beneath my hand it began to fade. Everything was fading, all colour and form were fading away.

Troubled, I looked down at myself and saw that in my other hand I still held the solid red snooker ball.

The surface of the ball was shiny, reflective, glistening like the eye of a cow. In it I could see my body, my face bending away — but nothing else. Looking round, I saw that the tables had now completely faded. I blinked, trying to make the hall come back, but nothing happened. So where was I? Still inside something, still in a room — but it was bigger. This was an immense space. Like an image forming on a negative, its floor began to appear — metal, it looked like. The same smoky grey metal cloud that had once stopped my car. A wispy trace of movement on its surface. Around me, the room was expanding, becoming so big that I had trouble keeping it in my head.

I checked — I still had the ball.

There was no furniture, or features, or patterns. No distinguishing marks. I stood in an immense open room, something built on an unearthly scale. And yet for some reason it felt familiar — there was something about it that still felt like the pool hall. Yes, somewhere Dusty Springfield was still singing, though I wasn't sure which song. I strained to hear the words. I still felt like me. I was Jack Grout — the words for that thought came into my head. *You are Jack Grout.* I was thinking about this when it occurred to me that the words had come from Dusty. Dusty had spoken. *You are Jack Grout.* I nodded in agreement. I was.

'Welcome, Jack.' In Dusty's husky voice, that strange, throaty voice, filled with ambiguity, I was being welcomed.

'Hi,' I said.

'You haven't been here for many years. Since you were nine years old.'

'No, that's right,' I said, speaking into the emptiness of the room. I just spoke normally, I figured I didn't need to shout. They have technologies.

But I didn't feel normal. It was Dusty's voice. Her voice

came right into my head. I felt all mixed up by it. I found Dusty, her speaking voice, so seductive. When she sings, Dusty soars, making clear, firm statements. 'All I See Is You.' Her speaking voice, on the other hand, had a catch in it, a smokiness that was both comforting and alluring. But I knew that this was all wrong — wasn't Dusty a lesbian? Plus she was dead. Anyway, this wasn't Dusty, this was the aliens. I knew that. But the aliens weren't talking formally any more. They were just . . . talking. It was hard to take. I mean, the aliens are supposed to sound alien.

'Jack, why d'you think we made contact with you, originally?'

I just wanted to listen to her, I didn't want to have to think. Until now this experience had just been a pleasant drift. But suddenly I was falling back through the years. Making an effort, I said, 'Why did you contact me? Well, it seemed like you were using me to look at our planet, weren't you? I had this idea that I was explaining the place to you.'

'Yes, that's correct,' whispered Dusty.

There was a pause, as though they were working out what to say next.

Then her voice came again. 'You were chosen at random, by chance. We looked through phone books and selected every millionth name.'

'All the phone books on earth?'

'Yes.'

'Wow.' I had this image of a telephone directory service, up there in the sky, books open, counting through names. 'So I'm one in a million, huh.'

'Yes, Jack.'

Did they think that this was impressive? I couldn't tell

from Dusty's voice, which had a tone that kept calling me on at the same time as it had no inflection. Sort of like a really sexy-sounding international toll operator — you're never going to meet her.

Now there was another of their pauses, like they were changing the software or something. I didn't mind this, it gave me a chance to work on myself. I found I was breathing hard. I guess it was a big deal for me, finally getting some info on things I'd been puzzling away at all my life.

I took the chance to get a question in. 'So have you been watching me?'

'We are not your god.' This time there was emotion. Dusty spoke firmly, perhaps with irritation even. I found irritation from them very frightening, it was hard not to cower. Standing alone in that giant room of theirs, everything was too big and too strange for me to feel that I had even the tiniest piece of control.

But I knew I mustn't waste this opportunity. 'So what are you?'

They had a pat answer waiting. 'You would say we were an alien species from outer space who are more technologically advanced.'

'I would say?'

'Human beings from what you call Earth would say. Human beings from the Earth's western world. That's how they describe us.'

'What would I say?'

'Well ... Jack ... Why would you ask us what you would say?'

Was that a laugh? So did they have a sense of humour? Sharing a laugh with them was just about overwhelming. It was too big! Also, it was so confusing when she said my name. Dusty's voice said my name as though it really appealed to her. This stirred me.

There was another of the pauses while something got figured out. I had this idea that there was a group of them, like a team — the Jack Grout team — who were gathered somewhere, pooling ideas and impressions. I didn't know where to look — were they above me? Dusty's voice, when it came, was everywhere, inside my head, yes, but in the air around me too, and in my bones, and my ear, and in my flesh, and in my groin. When Dusty spoke I was completely excited. I just wanted her to keep speaking to me.

The distinction between them and Dusty — this was really headache-making.

The pause got longer. It came into my head that they were waiting to see what I'd do. Putting the pressure on me. I didn't like this, it made me feel like a lab rat. And what could I do? I had the feeling I should be asking more questions, but there was an aspect to this that annoyed me — that they'd been watching me all these years and knew everything about me. And anyway — couldn't they hear what was going on in my head? But if they could listen in, Jack, they wouldn't have needed to bring you up here ... My thoughts began to tie me in knots and I wanted a way out. I had a small cognition — I remembered the snooker ball. Yes, it was there in my hand. Beautiful shining red thing. Was it just my imagination or was that ball alive? It seemed like an eye, watching me. Were they in there? An idea came into my head and immediately I acted on it. I stepped forward like a man playing lawn bowls and bowled that ball away across the floor.

Oh, to *do* something! It was sublime. And in that alien atmosphere the ball rolled so nicely. It seemed that the floor was perfectly smooth and frictionless — the ball rolled and rolled. I stood proudly, watching it get smaller. On and on the ball went, until finally I wasn't sure I really could see it any more.

I stood in the middle of their room, sort of defiant. I wondered what else I could do.

They still weren't talking, so I sat down and took my shoes off.

My feet felt great, the floor of their room was cool to my soles. I wriggled my toes. I stretched. I lay down. The pause went on and on. Were they watching to see what I'd do? I couldn't think of another meaningful action. I decided to keep talking.

'So, Dusty,' I said, 'how come you're working for these guys?'

She gave a little chuckle. It was throaty and I was knocked out that I had produced a noise like that in her. 'Jack,' she said, 'you know that this is only a projection of Dusty Spring-field's voice.'

'Yeah, I know, but it still has that effect on me.'

'We should apologise, Jack. We don't mean to keep you waiting. It's so important to get things right that we wait until we're sure. People have died. Thanks for your patience.'

'No worries, Dusty.' What did they mean, people have died? I wasn't sure I wanted to know. 'Maybe you guys should tell me a bit about yourselves.'

The response was so quick, I could tell they had this off pat. 'Jack, we don't feel it's wise for us to tell you anything about that.'

I was incredibly, profoundly disappointed. I knew right then that I wasn't going to see them. It was *so* frustrating. Before I knew it I was shouting. 'Look! Now I'm gonna live my life believing in you guys — and I don't even know what I'm believing in! I can't tell anyone about you — not because they'll think I'm nuts, but because there's nothing to tell. Come on! It's not fair!'

After a good long pause, Dusty's voice was sent to calm me. It came, both reasonable and seductive, into my body. 'That's true, Jack. We understand that. We agree.' Her agreement tingled inside me. 'That's why we brought you here today.'

'Okay. Okay, good.'

'We're afraid that if we show ourselves to you that you'll be harmed. You've read that book by Fred Hoyle, *The Black Cloud*. Remember what happened in that book?' As I remembered — a guy died because he couldn't handle the size of the alien intelligence he encountered — I realised that they were saying they knew I'd read that book. I remembered reading it — back when I was about eleven. This made me shiver.

'Yes, we do know you've read that book.'

My breathing came in short panting rushes — I'd had a sudden flash of what my life was going to be like when they put me back home.

'Calm yourself, Jack.'

How did they do that — have Dusty turn up the intimacy level? It was as though she touched the parts of me that other voices couldn't reach. In an effort to regain control, I sat up and concentrated on my breathing. I sensed now that they were genuinely concerned about me — that people had died here, and if I didn't improve they were going to break the contact. 'Sorry 'bout that,' I said, 'just struggling a bit here.'

'We understand. This is difficult. You're doing well.'

Was I? My head was on high rotate, trying to make what was happening to me now fit with the old version I had of my past. Had they been with me all the time? Had they been watching my every moment? Not God, they said — just all-seeing. Had they given me any privacy? Like, did they know about my smallness as a person — the times I'd been cruel, or cowardly, or selfish? I'd thought I was alone at these times, surely it wasn't fair to judge me if in fact I hadn't been? Though I knew as I thought this that it was pathetic.

Had they just watched? Or had they been able to listen in on my thoughts too?

'Jack, you seem to be accusing yourself. We haven't brought you here to judge you. Many people who come here are proud — that all their triumphs have not gone unnoticed. If it's any consolation to you, you seem to us to be a good person.'

'Harmless, right.'

'Yes.'

'Gee, thanks.' I was gutted. My life wasn't something I wanted on stage. Knowing that at least no one knows of your smallness, your pathetic inadequacy — that you alone have to live with yourself — surely that is one of the basic consolations.

'Jack,' they said — and now, although it was still Dusty's voice, which still induced those tinglings in my extremities, increasingly now it was them behind the voice that I was sensing — 'Jack, we are aware that our presence is a disturbance in the lives of the humans we've intruded upon. But we don't think it wise to show ourselves to you. One reason is, we're not sure exactly how we'd do that. Even if we could we don't think we would. But we're trying to offer something in compensation. That's why we've brought you here.'

I was working on my breathing, which was ragged.

'Could you put your shoes back on, please, Jack.'

I picked them up. 'What if I didn't?' I said.

'Well, they might be left here, and that would disturb the

nature of this space — when we collapsed it, it would have something left in it.'

'So what do you do with the bodies?'

'Which bodies?'

'Of the people that die.'

'We drop them in the ocean, Jack.'

'Cute.'

'What do you think we should do with them?'

'Dump them on the side of the road, like in a horror movie, with smoke coming out of their holes, and a weird patch of burnt grass all round them.'

'We've tried that.'

'Shit, have you?' I was standing now. 'That'd rark up the natives.'

'Yes, it did. We've also tried returning them, absolutely without trace. That didn't provide satisfaction either. Any ideas on this subject would be very welcome.'

I nodded. It was good to have something outside myself to think about — but as soon as I started thinking about Earth again, my head hurt. As though wanting to distract me, they said, 'Jack, please look behind you.'

At first there was nothing to see, just miles of floor stretching away. Then from the low distance I realised that something was coming. Something red. The snooker ball.

The ball came speeding towards me across the floor and went past and rolled on, tireless, into the vastness that lay ahead.

'Could you follow the ball, please, Jack.'

At first I walked. But that ball was really travelling and I broke into a jog. Soon I was sprinting. I was going so fast, I couldn't believe how fast I could run. It was kind of desperate, but exhilarating too. I seemed to be running out of myself, going so fast that I couldn't keep up.

Then in front of me I saw a doorway.

No building, no walls, no steps leading up to it, though it was the kind of grand doorway that would have steps — a massive doorway. But no door, just an oblong hole, a frame. The speed I was going meant that it was coming up quickly. I tried to slow. I must have looked like the Road Runner; my heels dug in, smoke came from my shoes. I lurched to a halt before a standing rectangle made of a sandy, weathered stone. It towered over me, a frame in space. There was nothing through it, or on either side. Then I looked up and saw that on the great stone balanced across its top was a flat panel, where letters were appearing. They faded up out of the sandy background, ornate in style. They said,

MUSEUM

8

The first association the word *museum* has for me is Shelley. She worked at the old National Museum, in Buckle Street in Wellington, for eight years, as an information officer. In dusty offices she wrote press releases, designed posters and arranged cocktail parties. The art wars, the museum biz rumbled all around her. Shelley just kept her head down and did her job. She always said she liked being in that big old building, with its dimly lit labyrinth of corridors, working amid the collection, which was housed in drawers, boxes, shelves, jars, racks and cabinets, in every room, along every passageway. It was as though she was clad, she said, in things, as though all the things of the world were on their way to the collection to form a kind of insurance against being forgotten. She said she would look at the mummy lying full length there in its glass room and imagine that she herself would some day be preserved, like a fish in a jar, and labelled, and kept. Allegedly she liked this idea. She said that working there made you have thoughts like that.

Then she was invited to join Te Papa.

Apparently that's what it was like — there was the old museum and there was Te Papa, and you had to join. She spent three months working with the new PR king, struggling to improve Te Papa's image. This was a couple of years before they opened and all anyone had to say about the place, especially the media, was that it was a disaster turning into a white elephant. She found that too tough and she transferred to the writing department, where she was one of the writers who wrote all the signs and labels in the place. Then she left, and went out into the market as a freelance writer. She's got a one-woman office in Ghuznee Street and a cellphone. She tries to walk to as many appointments as possible, and not to wear sunglasses, and to stay out of coffee bars. She seems to be making a go of it — even if ninety percent of her work does still come from Te Papa.

Shelley is the only writer I've ever heard of who doesn't feel she should be writing a novel. She doesn't leave poems, or bits of poems, around the place on scraps of paper or in the margins of books. She's not an artist. She writes good clear prose, she says, and semi-snappy headlines, and she always hits her deadlines. She doesn't stay up late agonising.

She is however inordinately proud of the words she wrote which are on display in Te Papa. She takes people, our friends, in for tours of the place and the tour they have to make is of Shelley's labels. 'That's very nice, Shell' — staring down at a couple of sentences about a bulging waistcoat that belonged to King Dick Seddon. 'So did you decide that this would be here?' pointing at the waistcoat. 'Did you design all this, Shell?'

'No, I just wrote the words,' says Shelley firmly.

Shelley was fond of family outings. She'd announce that tonight we were all going to a rerun of *Lawrence of Arabia* at the Embassy. Or off on an art-buying expedition. Or that we were going to sit on the top of Mount Vic in the Wolseley and plug our little TV into the cigarette lighter and drink beer and watch the Oscars. In fact we did do this, more than once. She'd use her cellphone to order pizza, which was delivered to our car, where we scoffed it, overlooking the city lights.

One Sunday she announced that we were having a tennis outing. This was in March, it had got colder, but it was the only time that that particular court was available. She'd managed to get hold of the key to a private court in Wadestown, up near the beginning of the town belt, which was collectively owned by a group of tennis nuts.

When we arrived, just before lunch, it wasn't cold, it was freezing. The court was an old one, asphalt, dark, with chipped lines and a net that hung limp and wrinkled, as though it was something left out to dry. Around the courts, tall pines blocked out most of the sun. A sharp little wind came in through the chinks between the trunks. The court itself was covered in pine needles. Only Pood's dog was excited — he ran in circles, barking.

'Aw, Mum,' said Stevie, disgusted.

At this time in his life it was hard to manage Stevie. For one thing, he was so big. He'd been lifting weights since he was fifteen, at the urging of his coach, who convinced him that if he ate steak and pumped iron he'd have the shoulders to power a serve the size of a bullet train. And now he'd made the regional team it really looked as though we might have to take his teenage dream of turning pro seriously. He was kind of full of himself, over-large, and, at the same time, over-modest, prone to be defeatist about his own abilities.

I was incredibly proud of him. Stevie, I know you'll read this some day. I'm incredibly proud of you.

Shelley . . .

Stevie mucked up our family games of tennis, though. We all play, with varying degrees of skill, and for years we'd been holding tournaments and battling for the coveted Grout Cup (cardboard). The Pood and Shelley were in charge of the handicapping and by doing this carefully they usually managed to engineer a gripping final — historically, between Lynley and Stevie. But then Stevie got too good. No one could return his serve, ever. For a while he played with his left hand but he got very frustrated — Stevie has a huge will to win. Lynley came up with the idea that as well as a handicap he would have to wear a skin-diver's weight belt to slow him down, but his coach nixed it. So the title had been allowed to go uncontested for over a year. But then Poodle had a new idea, which was that he would play tethered to a chair by a length of rope. If he served underarm, and if when he pulled the chair over he lost the point, if the rope was short enough so that he couldn't come to the net or reach the tramlines, then maybe . . .

But the dark court was covered in pine needles and it was bloody cold.

Shelley was undaunted. 'Stevie, get to work with that broom. You guys, stop shivering, look, the sun will be all through here in ten minutes — Donna, help me with this blanket. Jack, can you tie Elvis up, please.'

The rule was, you had to watch. We had camp chairs (and the wooden chair that was going to be tied to Stevie) and sat in a group and shouted. Once we got the first game going, between Shelley and Lynley, things warmed up.

It was a strange court. You don't get that many single courts, set all by themselves; it means you're always playing the feature match. The rusty wires, the asphalt, the chipped lines, the sound of the wind in the pines, it reminded me of the way the flax rattled at that hilltop court we used to play on at Pukerua Bay when I was a kid. There on the edge of the trees, it was as though somehow you had found a path that led out of the world.

The idea with the chair worked well, especially the rule that the chair wasn't allowed to fall over. Stevie lost to the Poodle for the first time in years. In a tight game, Lynley lost to Shelley on an Elvis (an Elvis is where you lose control of the ball and allow the damned dog to get it. Elvis, tied to the net post, refuses to give the ball up until it has been thoroughly slobbered. Penalty: two points.) I had to play Stevie without the chair. This match had, in the past, been a real high point of the tournament — father versus son, coach versus player — but these days it merely consisted of me watching the ball go screaming past in befuddled admiration. Every now and then there'd be a pause for Stevie to say something like, 'Jeez, Dad, if you're going to half-volley from there you've gotta go cross-court.' Taking a ball, he would model the stroke. Sometimes he would make me practise it. Lynley and Shelley would complain — 'Get on with it!' But the Poodle and I both indulged Stevie. Poodle competed with me to be his biggest fan. We were both in awe of his talent. To control the ball so effortlessly — it made you happy to see it.

How good was Stevie? It was a subject that Shelley frequently quizzed me on. Should we be encouraging him in this hopeless dream of turning professional and going out on the tour? It's not like he'd even been national age champion or something. Shelley would say, 'So how's he going to beat any of the international players?' Sitting there beneath the pines, this came up again. Stevie was playing Lynley now, taunting her with drop-shots and sliced balls that turned at right angles when they bounced. Poodle had taken Elvis for a walk. Shelley was beside me in one of the canvas chairs and she never took her eyes off him as she spoke.

'What if he goes out there and plays every day and he just always gets beaten? Stuck in Zagreb or somewhere. I dunno — Utah. Knocked out in the first round of the Skegness Open.' Her eyes followed him. 'There'll be no one around him, Jack.' Talking quietly so he wouldn't hear. 'Remember that time when his serve packed up and you played with him every night for a month — who'll do that?' Pausing while a noisy plane flew over. 'That's what your family does, doesn't it, it surrounds you, and Stevie's never won a game without us. We're there, just out of the picture. He always comes home to us and you talk him through it. Poodle plays Hearts with him. Lynley gives him heaps — he loves it. That's all the stuff that holds him together. Don't you think?'

Stevie seemed to be in trouble, running backwards, Lynley at the net — effortlessly he turned and smacked the ball down the line.

'And then I think: what would he be without that dream? Just some bloke at the office?'

'Like me,' I said.

Overhead, the sun had moved round now so that most of the court was brightly lit. But the trunks of the pines made a shadowy circle. Their higher branches groaned in the light breeze.

Shelley took my hand.

We sat side by side, hands linked, heads swivelling on our necks as we followed the ball. 'Go Lynley!' shouted Shelley. Lynley made a difficult get, dropped the ball near the tramline and smirked at Stevie as he strained helplessly at the end of his rope. Shelley and I broke into wild applause.

Shelley ferreted in her bag. 'You are just some bloke,' she said, passing me the sunblock. 'Aren't you. I'm just some woman you're married to. We just live in a house with our kids and we just get up and go to work. Sometimes I ask myself, So what do you want, to be on TV?'

There on the edge of the trees, the wires of the court made a room, an airlock between worlds, with us Grouts all showcased inside. Out on the asphalt the soles of Stevie's big white shoes slapped — it was a sound that echoed off the tree trunks. Looking up, I could see the fathomless blue of the sky. I stared out into those watery depths. I knew that if I stared hard enough and long enough I would see something. I dragged my eyes away. Just an ordinary bloke, I thought — if only I could make that true.

The other association the word *museum* has for me is of course Te Papa. I guess it's inevitable, what with Shelley working there. 'Redefining the word Museum' — she wrote that. And then the big opening. And then the condom. And then the critics. And then the two million visitors. Me, I like being in the place. Wandering round, finding things. It's the kind of outfit that makes everyone a critic. Everyone has an opinion. Wandering, thinking. It's not something I thought the nation would ever have, a strong opinion one way or the other about a cultural institution.

Thinking, So this is a museum.

9

MUSEUM

When I went beneath the word, my ears popped.

I stopped, listening. Nothing. When I glanced back I saw that the doorframe was no longer visible. I had the idea that it was still there, that if I retraced my steps I would find myself outside it again.

They hadn't spoken since they'd returned the snooker ball to me.

I thought that maybe I heard a skylark singing, but when I tried to pinpoint the sound I couldn't be sure. I strained to catch it. I had the sense that something was growing around me — that a background was being filled in. There was nothing to see and nothing to hear. There were no definite sensations of any sort. But somehow I seemed to be in company. When I tried to put a finger on it, it occurred to me that something familiar seemed to be there in the background. It was just a feeling I had, no more; I sat down to concentrate on it. But I found that that didn't help. I just had to relax and it was there. I was in the company of something. The longer I sat, the stronger the feeling got. It was an immensely familiar feeling, though one I'd never actually identified before. The company of New Zealand. I had the thought that the aliens came to this spot, and sat, and they got this feeling too — that this was the feeling of being in New Zealand, and that for them it was immensely strange, and wonderful.

I can't say what the feeling was. I mean, it wasn't like one of those Welcome to My World commercials or a TV One promo. It wasn't dripping pungas and baches and sacred cowsheds. It had those things in it, maybe, but faint, part of a mix. If you focused on it, it disappeared. It was just something that was there all the time in the background, and it made me think of a month I'd spent working up the back of my uncle's farm, pulling the ragwort by hand out of a gully paddock. Long days on my own. I kept thinking someone was watching me and I'd look around at the hills.

Now I noticed that on the floor beside my toe an object was appearing. I can't tell you what an astonishing sensation that was — to watch something arrive into being. First there was just a blur, like on *Star Trek*, when Scotty is beaming them up, and then it gained tangibility . . . gravity . . .

It was a rock. A stone. About the size of a hen's egg, but not as regular. Dark coloured. Nothing special — just an attractive stone you might find on a riverbank and put in your pocket. It sat there, near my toe.

I waited to see what would happen.

Nothing. The stone, and that feeling of company, and me sitting in the featureless place called Museum. I said out loud, 'Okay, what happens next?' There was no answer. So I picked up the stone.

It was just a stone. It sat inside my hand, quite comfortable. It was cold. I closed my fingers around it — and as my skin began to warm it, an intense sensation grew in me. The impression was that my face had come off. This is hard to describe. My face came off and it hung in the air in front of me so that I could look at it. But before I could get self-obsessed again I saw that something was filmed between me and my face, and as it grew clearer I saw that it was the face of a woman. It loomed, huge. It wasn't a fact, like the stone, it was an image, which was alive, with depth, and colour, and movement. It was a face that at first I didn't recognise. Then I remembered that I'd seen this face in photos. It was my mother. In the photos she was holding me — I was a baby.

It wasn't that she was gazing at me with love or anything. I mean, she was, I guess, but that wasn't the point. The point was her face, which was a language I knew how to speak brilliantly well. The planes of her face — the shape of her brow, and the shape of her chin, and the shape of her nose, and mouth, and lips. The Mount Rushmore of her face, the living landscape of it. The tone of her skin. Its wonderful colour. The meaning of the shape of her face — it was a map I could read.

And behind her face, or through it, was my face. Part of my fascination was with the way my face was a thing that had grown from hers. My face a variation of hers. Me a variation of her.

She must have been about twenty-one.

You don't get to see faces like this, not unless people are dead, or asleep, and if you see them at those times they're missing the presence that being alive gives them. You never see your parents' faces. You only see what those faces are saying. I remember once I'd been living in England for about three years and then my dad was sent to a conference in Boston and he said he could fly home through London and would I like to meet him? I went out to Heathrow in good time, and stood at the appointed gate at the appointed hour, and waited. Streams of people were coming through the concourse, and I was looking for him. Plane after plane had landed, and I searched through the faces.

The arrival time came and went and still I couldn't see him. Now I knew my dad, and I knew he wouldn't leave the airport without finding me. If I'd missed him, I should stay where I was, because he would figure out where I would most likely be and then search for me there. So I stayed where I was in the crowd at the barrier and just kept looking at those oncoming faces. It was tiring, searching through them all.

Four hours passed. I can't believe now that I stayed there so long, but there is something dogged in me and that was typical, to have just stayed there. I knew that he would find me, or else he'd send a message on the Tannoy. I stood on and on, in that throng of people, who came and went in shifts around me, meeting their loved ones, and my eyes crawled over the faces. And then a face appeared in among them, a face I hadn't seen for three years. But what was so strange was that it didn't look anything like the way I remembered. The forehead was at a different slope. The nose came out at an interesting angle. The mouth, the skin tone — it wasn't what I remembered at all. Slowly, inside my head, a knowledge was forming — this one might fit the pattern. And after what seemed like a long time my mouth moved and I was calling out, 'George Grout!' He turned and found me.

As we sat on the bus back to town I watched his real face return. It took about two hours, and then I couldn't see the structure I'd seen at the airport any more. It came to me then that I didn't have a clue what my father looked like — I only ever knew what his expression was. Was he angry, was he pleased? I could read his expression with every grain of intelligence that I had. Of everything in the world, the meaning of my father's face was one of the things I knew most about.

All of this passed through my head as I sat there with the stone in my hand. Thinking, This is what should be in museums. Faces, and smells, and words, and touches.

There in the aliens' museum.

The faces of the women, nurses and family friends who held the baby of me at the small country hospital where I'd been born, these faces were now faded in and out before my eyes.

Then some faces from my childhood began to appear. I grew up in the sticks and the people we knew were farmers. Here was Colin Cahey, who lived along the road. This face was so different from Dad's — it was always whiskery, and it had so much red in it. It was huge — Colin was a big man, with a big lump of head. The way that hairs grew out of that head — as a child, this fascinated me. The wires that came out of the ears. The way the hairs of the eyebrows didn't lie sideways like my dad's but came jutting out, like carrot fronds sprouting from the ground, so that the eyebrows made a limp veranda over the eyes. The eyes themselves, which seemed to have a curtain of water running continually down them, making a smile-shaped pool along their bottom rim.

Colin's face floated there before me and then I saw his wife, Mary Cahey, and all the little Caheys — they were Catholics and there were nine kids, all variations on Colin and Mary. I saw them all, perfectly, the faces of those kids I hadn't given a thought to for years. I knew the names of every one. But I wasn't interested in the names, not then. I was seeing how my experience of faces had been gained — the order that faces had come to me. It was as though somehow I had been placed at the bottom of a midden, seeing up through it — seeing the things on which the stuff at the surface had been built.

Because it's the first thing you see, isn't it, a face, and you read the hell out of it with extraordinary expertise, just immediately. What you know after one quick glance — it's primary knowledge.

There in the aliens' museum.

Now I was seeing all the kids in my primers class from forty years before. The kid who ate a spider for a bet. The kid who pissed on the classroom floor. Fatty Clarke, who said, It's all a big laugh, mate. Ian French, who was little — his face said, I know I'm a shrimp, but if you chase me I'll dodge and wriggle and always get away. Helen Moody, who said, I don't know why you keep doing the stupid things that everybody else does.

As these faces came, I could feel my own face coming too. It was growing on the front of my head. I could feel its forehead swelling and its skin being shaped. I could feel a strain on it, as I tried to make it do what I wanted, as I tried to meet the faces that were coming towards mine. I was a puzzled boy — my frown line was working its way into my forehead. Well, I was the only one who had encountered the aliens and I looked everywhere for another face that had seen what I had.

Then those faces that had been in Mr Deeble's class with me, in Standard Three and Four. He went round the room, making us say what we were going to be when we grew up. Those faces, tilted towards the future. Andrew Heggie, dead now — I am going blind into the unknown, his face said, and then he drowned himself when he was nineteen, swimming out into the harbour, leaving his clothes above the high-water mark. Stephen Grant, who had a car accident — bang! Gloria Stacey, who followed her face onto the stage. The face with the Gorbachev mark down the side of it. The face with the scar. The face that was always searching the ground, the one that looked up towards the light. That was plain Nancy Winch, who became a nun — I met her years later, on a bus, and the peace of her made me consider religion for the first time.

Those faces that are masks, that never change. That are held like shields — not hard, because they are made of soft flesh, but you can never remember that, can you, when you are looking into them and finding them so still, so able not to react to you. To control your face, to steer it before you, through the world like a woman on the bow of a ship, to let it make your way — that was never my face.

Now the terrible faces of my teenage years began to stream towards me. They sorted me out. I felt a pain in my jawbone and realised that my teeth were aching. Grind, grind, like Jake Heke. Such a stressful time. Where was the face for me? My girlfriends' faces bloomed slowly. Here was Frances, who I never dared to kiss. For three whole days she liked me. Then she saw I was too timid for her. Suddenly her face was averted from me and all I ever saw was the back of her head, curls flouncing as she hurried away. I tingled with pride at how pretty she was. It came to me then that there is a pecking order of faces — that we let those who are beautiful have power they don't seem to deserve. They are closer to the centre — they'll be okay in the bright light which shines there. These thoughts arrived in my head there in the aliens' museum and have never left. So is that what the aliens' studies had told them about the human race? That we follow our faces? That in our construction of the world, faces come first?

But if we're talking about what makes us go, what about love? Okay. Okay, what about the indomitable human spirit, that stretches our species into every corner of the unknown, to bring new possibilities back to us?

Now that voice of Dusty Springfield's came into my head again, saying, 'Jack, we don't have faces.'

I sat there, stupefied by the thought. An image of a blob came into my mind, a smooth bulb, made of flesh, like one cheek of a bum, maybe lightly covered with hair. What is a face? That it has expression? 'So what do you have instead?' I said.

But there were no more words.

I said, 'You can't just leave me with that!' I protested, I begged, I insisted. I said I had a horrible picture of them in my mind and I wanted something to replace it. 'Don't leave me this way!' I said. I was nauseated.

I was also — I have to say this — proud. Isn't it dumb. But I had images then that seemed to billow like balloons — Greta Garbo's face, huge and pale and filling a giant screen. This face rose in me like some piece of profound evidence. The Statue of Liberty, its face high above the water. Don Bradman, Muddy Waters, Amelia Earhart. Where on earth did those faces come from, that I'd never thought about before? But suddenly they were there, like trump cards I was playing. We fabulous humans. Belmondo, Deneuve, Liv Ullman — what are the movies but temples to our faces?

I began to think back on all the great film faces I'd seen but they moved me on by putting in front of me the first girl I ever kissed. Diane Firth — where are you now? Hello, Bronwyn, hello, Jenny, hello, Claire. A girl for each year at high school — or bit of each year; there were long gaps. Then here came Mary, who had an extraordinary face that looked like it should be in a silent film. I couldn't believe that a face like that could look on me with affection. Well — you don't want to hear me maundering on about my old girlfriends. But I was astonished to see them — to see how casually I had looked at them. I hardly knew their faces at all! When there was so much written there. But you couldn't look at your girlfriends. That would have been intimate. They were beside you when you walked, or you were kissing them. You couldn't see them.

Then the faces I had at least partly seen started to come. The ones that had arrived as I edged into adulthood — or what passes for adulthood with me. Now the faces began to tell me stories and I liked to look at them if I could. When I worked behind a counter for six months in England, serving the public, I would stand while they wrote their cheques and see their skin and their brows and their mouths and the way their noses were shaped. All so astonishingly different.

It occurs to me now that the aliens may have found it useful for me to look in this way.

Then the faces that I knew well began to arrive. My parents, seen in adulthood. My first wife — how come I couldn't see that we would never last? Then Shelley, all freckles and teeth, who I liked to look at in the dark, and in the morning, and across the dinner table.

And finally the faces of my kids. They really are the only faces we're allowed to gaze into without resistance. We stare and see ourselves, and slowly we see them. Those soft lines, gradually falling away. The features which emerge. Stevie with a small brown spot which I noticed one day just above his left eyebrow. How long had that been there? Always, said Shelley — so I didn't gaze *that* well, did I. But from that day forward I always looked for that spot, to make sure it was really him. A spot or a wart or a mole or a line or a strange flattening — how often now I notice that a face has a hollow or a bump where it might not be expected, on a cheek or on the brow. These points we focus on with such tender interest.

10

A long strange trip — then when I returned to myself I was back in the pool hall.

I waited through the early morning until the locksmith came, then hung a sign on the street door that said, 'Closed due to family illness,' and drove home.

My teeth ached. My eyes peered out through the windscreen as though I was looking into a snow storm. My arms, limp ropes, hung off the steering wheel. I just wanted to get into bed.

There was no one in the house. I struggled my way out of my clothes and pulled the blankets around me.

When they found me I can't have looked too good — I surfaced at twilight to a family committee standing round the bed. Shelley, and Lynley, and Donna, who we call the Poodle, and big Stevie hanging round the fringes, not really part of this. The women all looked concerned.

I didn't know what to tell them.

They brought me cups of tea, and a hottie. The Poodle sat on the end of the bed and studied me. I could hear the sounds of the others in the house, their feet on the floors. The TV voices came through from the front room. I said I'd just felt tired after having to go down in the middle of the night. I said I'd just felt like having a sleep.

This raised huge alarm. A year or so earlier I'd had a cancer scare, a lump cut out of me that proved to be malignant. What if this was cancer tiredness? I tried to smile and say, it's nothing.

But no one was fooled. Something had happened to me

— everyone could see that. A weight lay inside me, a soggy mess, like a ton of wet newspaper, a mass of memories.

The Poodle was hanging up my clothes when she found something in the pocket of my trousers. The red snooker ball.

In the museum of the aliens, as the last face began to fade before my eyes I felt a weight in my hand. Looking down, I saw I was still holding the stone. It was cooling — it'd had the warmth of all those people, all their faces in it, and now it was fading back to stony silence. It got colder and colder, my palm shrank from it, and yet it began to glow. From stone-grey it turned brown and then orange and then gradually it became red. This disturbed me, it wasn't right — red was a hot colour, cold things should be white. But the red got redder, until it was a bright, shiny primary colour. Smooth surfaced. A cold red snooker ball, chilly and meaningless, lying mute in my hand.

When I looked around I was back in the pool hall, sitting on the floor, down among the table legs. The aliens had withdrawn.

All they'd left me with was the knowledge that they existed.

What's the matter with Dad? I could all but hear the kids saying it. I could feel their worry. And yet I couldn't tell them. You imagine going out and saying to your best-beloved: Hey, everybody, guess what — last night I was abducted by aliens!

That night Shelley eased her way into our bed as though she wasn't sure she should be disturbing me. I pretended to sleep. But this pretence is always such a hammy thing, isn't it, with such a huge effort required to keep your breathing regular

— in ten seconds you're absolutely wide awake. I reached out a hand towards her.

She turned in the bed and gave me her full attention. 'Hello, Bedrest,' she said.

'Hello, Gorgeous.'

'Feeling okay?'

Gorgeous. Honey. Darling. These names can sound so ugly. Darling, just make me a cup of tea, would you. And then suddenly it comes out right, so natural, and you feel that every atom in the universe is in its perfect place. You're home and living in love. But, ugly or right, these names aren't things you want other people to hear. The aliens, for example. I could sense them in our bedroom, up there in the light fitting, observing. 'Now the human male addresses his mate with one of the alternative names that the humans use to convey personal warmth, an exclusive relationship. This phenomenon has been observed in every human culture we have studied . . . now it seems likely that a moment of intimacy will occur . . .'

'It's probably just the weather or something,' I said. 'I fell asleep down at the pool hall and when I woke up I felt like shit. I just came home and got into bed.'

Now the male human is denying that he has had an off-planet experience.

Shelley was thoughtful. After a moment she said, 'D'you think it's the cancer?'

'No.'

'Will you see the oncologist?'

'Only if it happens again.'

'When's your next appointment?'

'About a month.'

Shelley has a way of looking at you where she tilts her

brow towards you and then seems to look at you from under it, a kind of deadeye. It's a very steady gaze. I've seen her give it to a guy with a gang patch, to legions of smart-mouths, to our kids — to pretty much everyone she knows at some stage. It's a gaze that says, I don't mind squaring up to you. She follows the opening look with a small movement — her brow goes back and suddenly she's looking at you full face. Not down her nose (it's a lovely nose, longish, slimmish, a shapely nose that is almost never out of joint. I love that nose, the way it divides the air) but straight on. Not hiding behind anything. Giving you her open eyes.

I could feel that gaze on me there in the still of the night.

This had been an awkward time for us. We were still in the shadow of me having bought the pool hall without consulting her and Shelley was only part-way to readmitting me to the index of acceptable people. My impression was that I'd been given some rope because of the cancer scare — but only some.

Not that I'm afraid of Shelley. I've met her gaze. My life with her means everything to me, but, you know, vice versa, or what are we doing together?

'Mum and Dad have been together forty-nine years.'

'What makes you suddenly bring that up?' she said. 'Don't you think we're going to make it?'

'We might make it. You'll probably leave me, when I lose my mind. Then you'll find you love me beyond all reason and that life is meaningless without me, and I'll prepare a bed of hot coals for you to walk across and you'll have been to one of those new-age courses where they teach you to conquer your fear by walking across hot coals and you do it in a canter and we'll be reunited to the sound of distant bells and hairy-chested men rejoicing in the valleys. You'll have accepted me for what I am and we'll be all set for another decade of happiness, relatively speaking.' I spun the words. 'Which will be lived among flowers, beds of tulips, and lilies, and clinging clematis vines.'

'What are you on?' she said. But I'd distracted her.

'I had a dream about Mum,' I said, going on as though this was all going to be connected. 'One of those dreams full of faces, and there was this one face, I couldn't put my finger on it, it was someone I knew, really well, and then I realised it was her, the face she had on in my baby photos. She must've been about twenty-one, twenty-two.'

'The face she had on.'

We lay there in the dark house, side by side, with the kids at various stations around us, like three points of the compass. You could hear your life going by, tick, tick, the sounds of the old wooden house settling down for the night.

'I just couldn't help thinking,' I said, 'about how that was her face then, and she had all those years in front of her, and now she's had the years, and you look at the one face and then the other face and you try and understand what's in between. That's all.'

Shelley didn't say anything. She didn't even make a little noise to indicate that she recognised that I'd said my bit and now it was her turn. I thought, Don't say any more, Jack. Don't move.

A car went by, down on the road, some hoon, horn wailing in the middle of the night.

A long silence followed, and then when I eased myself up to look at her I saw that her eyes were closed. Her breathing was slow and very calm. I lifted myself on an elbow and tried to see her in the dark. Dear Shelley. I couldn't see very well and I had to remember her face, the wispy frame her hair made around it, and the elegant nose, and the freckles. I tried to imagine knowing her without knowing what she looked like. I tried to imagine her not having a face, and whether she would be her without a face. No door. No windows. The person in there somewhere but you couldn't see what they were giving you.

I wanted to tell the aliens, however, that they shouldn't isolate faces out — that faces go with bodies and that what's in the faces is what's in bodies, which is being, which is aliveness. That faces aren't masks. They seemed to have made faces the most important thing in their museum and I saw that for them it might be so, since they didn't have any. But that for us, the most important thing was . . .

I tried to decide. I lay there in the dark, looking down on Shelley's face with my night eyes, seeing the way the faint light in the room seemed to collect on her brow, which had a curve like a long arc of pale sand, some private bay where the waves came sliding in and where a foot had never trod. 'The most important thing is the way that things seem . . .' I said. 'The way that things seem.'

I was turning this thought over, wondering how you'd make a museum of it, when I realised that Shelley had her eyes open and was looking at me.

11

Down at the pool hall the balls rolled across the green tables, and formed clusters, and clicked against each other, and came to rest. The smoke rose from the cigarettes and made a layer that drifted towards the fans. The music fell from the speakers — business as usual. But I wasn't playing Dusty Springfield's greatest hits these days.

I sat behind the desk and studied the hall from the alien angle. The humans come here to study geometry — they come to calculate angles in their heads. They come here to make smoke come out of the sticks they put in their faces. They gather to drink something called Coca Cola. Yeah, but the aliens are smarter than that. They know what's going on. Okay, so how smart? I'd been trying to figure the appeal of pool halls for years and I wasn't sure. It's how things seem. A pool hall is a place that isn't anywhere — I think that is its real appeal. You aren't at work and you aren't at home. You aren't at the pub with every other loser. You aren't having a stylish coffee in some stylish cafe. And you aren't at the tennis club where you have to work up a huge sweat or lose ignominiously and brood about it for days. No, you're nowhere, and if you've got half a brain you turn off your cellphone so no one can reach you, and sink deep into the lost moment. That was why I was so careful about the music I played, and about the changes I made to the place, and about keeping it clean, and about replacing any light bulbs, and about the way I spoke to the guys. The way things seem. Did the aliens understand the importance of this?

The great thing about the pool hall had always been that

I didn't have to use my brain to run it, and so my thoughts could wander. I spent my days in long wobbling bubbles of time, filled with sunlight and drifting — when they popped I had no idea where I'd been. Magic. But now, with the aliens to think about, the place provided no distraction. I was *obsessed*. While the minutes trickled past, while the players came and went, I sat on my stool behind the counter and tried to figure it.

The aliens had a museum, that's what they called it — well, that was the name they'd shown me — a name from Earth, in English, in my language . . . so what did they call it in their language? And was it a museum to them, or was that just the way they'd presented it to me so that I'd understand it? And in the museum was a file, a kind of register, with all the faces I'd ever seen in it. So did that mean that the aliens were with me all the time? Or did it mean that in the tiny cupboards in the back corners of my brain I stored every moment of my life, every face, which they downloaded when I visited them? But I hadn't visited them for ages. But — yes — I did stick my head up through their cloud, on the day they stopped my car. But that wasn't long enough, surely?

Maybe my experiencing all those faces was the download?

And just inside the door of their museum there was a lobby where New Zealand came through — a place where this country was evoked. I couldn't figure what means they'd used, but they'd got it right. Which showed how smart they were.

So, a museum of New Zealand, in which there was a section devoted to me. I was one in a million, and there were three, nearly four million New Zealanders, so presumably there were three, three and a half of us in there. A Maori, a woman, an All Black, and a halfwit — it was probably something like that. Guess which one you are, Jack.

I sat behind the counter in the pool hall and wondered who these other New Zealanders were. Put an ad in the paper?

And if there was a museum of New Zealand, presumably there was a museum of Australia, and France, and Greenland, and Tibet, and San Marino. And if they'd made these museums by studying one in a million, and there were five billion people on the planet, that meant — I got my calculator out — that there were five thousand of us. Hell, Jack, you should be bumping into another abductee every other day . . .

While the snooker balls rolled and the smoke drifted, I obsessed. I was one in a million, good. But there were five thousand people like me on the planet. Wow, that was a lot. That was the entire audience of the Eric Clapton concert I went to — I wondered if I'd met five thousand people, face to face, in my whole life?

I began trying to think back over everyone I'd ever met.

If there were five thousand, that accounted for the UFO books and so forth. Everyone that was abducted was so overwhelmed they just had to write a book about it (well, me too, I guess). All those TV programmes about the Roswell encounter. Not that I watch them — those things are junk! I only ever watched enough to see if they were describing an experience like mine — which they weren't. But maybe the aliens had presented the encounter differently to everyone? Or maybe they'd just presented it differently to me? Because all the alien abduction books I'd ever read (glanced at, flicked through! — I swear!) had described really similar things. Little green men with almond-shaped eyes, flying them away in UFOs shaped like cigars. That was just so banal.

And did they only pick humans? I mean, we can't talk to the insects, but maybe they can? Those little insect heads — what's inside them?

And then I'd start thinking about all the times I'd presumed I was on my own. Sitting there behind my desk in the pool hall, with the guys moving round the tables in the shadows, like burglars, and the smoke curling under the lights, and the silent rolling of the balls — I'd suddenly remember: that time when you fucked Gloria McQueen when she was flat-out drunk. That was cute, Jack. And when you calmly told Nicky Steele that you were madly in love with Shelley — cruel. All my little cruelties, known about. My pettiness. My sneaking meanness. And my humiliations — only endurable because no one else knew about them. The despair, the common or garden despair.

It was like finding that God was watching after all.

It was also during this period that I ran the Wolseley into the back of another car. The Wolseley doesn't bend, but it cost $480 to reshape the back of that tinny Honda. This was the first time that a car I was driving had so much as touched another vehicle in eighteen years. Then I stared at some new bloke's face once too often at the pool hall and he offered to hang a punch on me. In the end the guys dragged him away, so the outcome was this feeling of solidarity. But who was the geek who didn't know how to act?

Shelley quietly informed me that for the second time in a week I'd polished off the milk before the kids'd had breakfast.

As I said, I don't have any truck with God, but I began to think what it must have been like back in the dark ages, when they really believed He was just up there through the ceiling and had His eye on them all the time. Watching TV, I kept thinking, So what do they make of this? So much of it is shameful. I mean, the aliens listening to our politicians — it doesn't bear thinking about.

1 2

I knew this blind guy once, who told me that he gradually lost his sight during his teenage years. It turned out he had some disease of the eyes — but he didn't know that then. He said that all he knew was that doing it made you go blind, but that he just couldn't help himself.

The poor suffering bastard. He came to mind during the period that followed my first visit to the aliens' museum. I knew that thinking about the aliens would ruin my life, but I just couldn't stop it. A kind of pressure began to build. Then one night I rang Shelley and said I was stopping off at Fatty Clark's for a drink. He'd come down to the pool hall, I said, and talked me into it.

Later, I rang her and said I was over the limit and was going to sleep on his couch. She offered to come and get me, so I said that Fatty and I were having such a great time, I wanted to stick with it. Okay, fine, she said. I had the league on the TV turned up loud, and the radio commentary too, and I clinked my glass against the phone so that the ice in it could be heard. Clink, clink, but I could tell she didn't believe me. 'Love you, Shelley,' I said, and she smiled dutifully down the phone.

It was like being unfaithful. I turned down the TV, turned the radio off, poured the ice-water out of my glass. I was sitting on the bed in a twelfth-floor room of the Hotel Raffaele on Oriental Parade. I *was* being unfaithful. I was devoting myself to someone else — me. But I couldn't help it. I had to go back.

I knew that the biggest risk was that I was being so

deliberate about this that I wouldn't get off to sleep. So I had planned my evening. I rang down for extra milk — milk drinks were what I needed at bedtime. I would go for a strenuous walk in the Roseneath hills. I'd brought along a book that had been putting me to sleep for months, *Suttree*, by Cormac McCarthy. I'd read a novel of his that I'd loved, *All the Pretty Horses*, but this one was just sludge. And I had the electric blanket turned to 1 — not too hot, not too cold. Just lukewarm, and cosy.

Great plan. But — none of it worked. At 2.45am I was out of bed and slumped in an armchair in a twelfth-floor room of the Raffaele, glumly confronting the infomercials. Bleary-eyed, exhausted — but awake.

'. . . and the astonishing thing about the new PoSola lenses is the way they cut the glare at the same time as really bringing the colours out of the view. Charlene, tell the viewers what new PoSola have done for you!'

At some point I realised I might have dropped off. Just for a moment. My neck was sore. Blinking, I looked around. '. . . and I just found PoSola really made a difference to my headaches . . .' Thank you, Charlene. Then it came to me that the TV seemed to be floating.

Struggling up, I crossed the room, drew the curtains, and looked out the balcony door. The harbour was still a shimmering semicircle — but now it was below me. I was rising. I could see Wellington laid out, suburb by suburb, and the dog-legging roads which connected it picked out in streetlights. When I turned back to look at the room, everything in it was loosed from its moorings. The bed floated up in the air as though it was a dinghy on a rising tide. I slumped into the armchair again, stupefied. The picture on the TV was reduced to snow. The motel room was a cube, rising into the sky, with me inside it.

The snow on that TV was fascinating. I'd never seen anything like it. I sat back in my chair, which seemed to be on gimbals, and stared at the patterns as though I was stoned. It was snow, all right. Not the there's-no-signal pattern — there was white stuff drifting, actual flakes of it, falling in a three-D curtain across a dark background. Snow was accumulating at the bottom of the picture in a solid bank. Then I saw that flakes were falling from the screen and coming out into the room. A white drift began to form around the base of the set. I shivered — the temperature was falling.

A flurry of snow went across the room on the city-side, and I saw that the door to the balcony appeared to be open — surely I'd closed it? — so that the snow which was filling the night was coming in, chilly and damp. The air was piercingly cold as it went into my lungs. Drifts were forming along the tops of every surface, and the floor was becoming mushy. I was cold! I considered going to the wardrobe for my coat but thought I might not make it.

I sat facing the doorway and now as I stared into the oncoming snow I could see that the frame of the door was rising to tower over me — a frame of stone. On the stone pediment, in large, serious letters, a word was carved:

MUSEUM

When finally I made it to the threshold all I could see inside the museum was darkness. No snow — it seemed that the snow stopped just inside the doorway. I have to say that the darkness in there didn't look inviting, it was so total. But I had no real thought of staying outside — this is what I'd come for. So through the door I went.

The air was clear. The wind was behind me. I stood, shivering in my shirtsleeves, in the darkness, waiting for the details of the museum to emerge. I was rather looking forward to the moment that felt like this-is-New Zealand, which was, I knew, just there somewhere inside the door. I shifted my position slightly, hoping to come upon it. In my memory it was warm — I was looking for warmth. But all I could find was darkness. My eyes were adjusted to the dark now. But still there was nothing to see.

I've never been that keen on the dark. I've gone forward into it with my hands held out, feeling my way, my heart bumping and ready to jump.

That's what I did now — put my arms out. I couldn't feel anything. I leaned forward, groping. Nothing. I shuffled a few steps. Still nothing.

When I looked back I had travelled a long way from the lighted doorway. I could see it, faint, behind me. As I watched, it appeared to recede. So was I moving even as I stood still? Where were the aliens? I tried to say that out loud: Where are you? But I wasn't able make a sound. Had my lips moved?

I held as still as I could, tried to breathe as shallowly as possible. The sense that I had any influence over these matters was fading fast, as was my sense that I existed at all.

The darkness grew, like some huge gravitational force that was increasing to squeeze me down to a frightened little dot. The darkness had grown over me, so that I felt as though I was inside a mountain.

I took a step forward. It was just a step, but it produced a pale glow, like a dawn, directly ahead. It seemed I would take five thousand steps to reach that light. By the time I did I would have lost all sense of where the entrance was. But now when I looked back the great doorway was gone. This didn't surprise me. I knew that I was in a nightmare and was just going to have to struggle my way through it.

As I trudged there was no moon, no stars, no distant brightness of city. No company at all. Just that pale distant glow, which, from time to time, seemed to disappear, so that I was lost again.

As I went my imagination groped forward. Was the brightness an island? With swaying palm and girl? Another doorway? A crowd of aliens, holding flickering torches?

Then as I came closer I saw that there was something square about the light. It was brighter towards the bottom, but top corners could be made out, and a line that joined them. A square city. A giant rectangular frame of light, in which the aliens lived. I was going to meet them. Then I saw that I'd got the perspective wrong, that in fact I was much closer than I had understood — that there was a square but that it was only a metre by a metre — that what I was looking at was something small, just a few strides away. I was hugely disappointed.

It was a museum case, not unlike the glass cases I had seen at Te Papa, with a dark base and a square of light; the light came from below to highlight whatever was being displayed. What that was, I couldn't see. Something flat, maybe a piece of paper. The Treaty of Waitangi or something? I felt a slight disappointment — this wasn't going to be about me at all.

Then I was over the case and looking down into it. The artefact was flat all right — a squashed hedgehog, lying on what looked like a strip of tar-sealed road. It was old — I was really pleased that I couldn't smell it. But, the instant I had that thought, the smell broke through. It was as though, innocent, I had put my nose right up close to that stinking thing and sucked in a massive lungful of it. I reeled back, gagging.

Further on, I saw that there was another case. I cast a hurried glance at the one I'd just been looking at — no sign, no label, nothing more to see — then set off towards this new destination.

I wasn't happy. All my alien experiences had been pleasant. Now I had that featureless darkness in me, like a test sample of death, and also now the dead-hedgehog pong — that stink had lodged in my nose, I couldn't get rid of it.

The second case had another hedgehog. This one had just been bowled; its guts lay, white like damp pasta, in a dark ooze of blood.

I tried to make myself look at it, but, honest, it was a struggle. Why had the aliens put *this* here? And where the hell was Dusty? But as I stood there shivering I heard something that cheered me. I could hear a bird singing — a skylark. Then a wash of memory passed through me — just a moment and it was gone. I remembered being beside this hedgehog, on a tar-sealed road, out in the sticks somewhere, with a skylark singing overhead. Instantly the sensation faded. But I was left with the thought: this is all from my memory. That must have been in Rataono, when I was just a kid.

This bit of the museum . . . is about my death?

The next case turned out not to be a case at all. It was just a pair of fist-grips, like a motorbike, mounted on a plinth, with a mould to put your face in. I had a gloomy certainty that the mould would fit my face perfectly — that I was going to have to stick my face right into some dead thing. Great.

But there was nothing else to do. When I peered around, all I could see was acres of nothing. Big darkness. And if I paused to think, the cold got to me something terrible. So I just plunged my face right on in.

Because of the motorbike handles, I expected a fast ride. But instead what I saw was a little theatre, a kind of dinky home cinema. Red velvet curtains parted. I remembered those red curtains. Behind them stood a little boy, in shorts and oxblood leather shoes. I remembered those shoes, they pinched my feet. He was clutching a ticket and a packet of Smokers. I watched this little bloke, peering round at everyone to see what he was supposed to do. It was all very simple. He was happy — he was going to the pictures. Little Jack Grout, aged about five. A regular sandboy. It cheered me right up to see that compact, uncomplicated little chap.

Accompanied by me, and by the aliens, the sandboy went into the cinema — the Starlight, I remembered — and sat down in the big seat to watch. He had to kneel on the front edge of the seat to see over the kids in front. It was *Bambi*. Disney colours, looking a bit primary to today's eyes. Schmaltzy music telling the emotions. The cutesy dialogue — 'Pwetty fwower.' Bambi's mother, with that dream-mother voice. Then the hunters. Then the gun. Then the bang, and Bambi's mother dying. Bambi's mother dying — that wasn't possible. For your mother to be dying and then for her to be dead.

Now the little theatre was filled with the face of my mother. She wasn't smiling at me. She had told me something and was looking to see if I understood. She was concerned that I had grasped a fact. My mother's great big face — even for a second time in a month, it was astonishing to see it so young. So alive. My mother is still alive, and going strong — she's seventy-something. Hi, Mum. But here was the little boy Jack trying to get his head around the idea that your mother could die.

It was unthinkable.

Now another memory entered from off to the side — a

woman friend of mine who had told me that her six-year-old daughter had asked to go and look in a cemetery. During the visit the girl didn't say too much. Then the next day she said, 'When you're dead, Mummy, I want there to be a little door, so I can just come through for a visit.'

The meaning of never.

Little Jack didn't want his mother looking at him like that. He wanted to stay close to her, to make sure she didn't get away. He cried.

Inside the little theatre I saw now that, as boy Jack went along his path, there was a blur in the wings, on either side, just offstage, and when I cast a glance that way I saw that things were lying stiffly there, passing on a kind of conveyor belt — sheep, possums, birds, fish dying on the thwarts, the odd cow with legs pointing at the sky, a bloated horse, a phalanx of hedgehogs — all the dead things I had ever seen, passing like a grisly verge on either side of my life. My gran. My other gran. The mother of my flatmate Arapata, lying in her coffin on the paepae. Andy Richmond, who took poison. A traffic accident victim, whose name I found later in the paper, Ian David Stent, I'd seen him all smashed up on the side of the road — and me driving carefully down the middle of my life, eyes averted.

I lifted my face away and stood there gasping, as though I had to suck life back into me. Those images, which I'd seen and then buried, that knowledge which I'd been so careful to avoid knowing — it was in me now, like cancer.

There was nothing to do but trudge on. Dead beat, dead beat, and the bottom falling out of everything.

Except that here now something else was forming. I realised that an object was appearing on my left. Thank god for a distraction. I was passing alongside a barrier — a wall.

No, a fence. A wooden fence, as high as my head, and each broad board of it undercoated in white. I dragged my fingers over its splintery surface and, as though the touch was a clue, began to remember. Now suddenly, after all that death, here was a reason to smile.

Carefully I explored ahead and, sure enough, set on the ground was an open tin of paint and a brush tipped in brown. Why anyone would choose to paint a fence chocolate brown I wouldn't know but when I was sixteen it was the colour that the Shearers, our neighbours, had selected, and so for my summer job that year, which must have been around 1967, I had painted every board of that long high fence three times over. The sun shone. There was no one around. There in the suburbs I kneeled on their green lawn and stroked coats of paint onto those warm, broad boards. For company I had a tiny transistor, cased in brown leather, a slightly darker brown than the paint, and even now that transistor, sitting on a shelf in my shed, has chocolate brown spots on it.

The museum had warmed up. Grinning now, I took the brush and began to paint. The paint was wonderfully wet, thick, fecund even — I wasn't sure the aliens had got it quite right. Nevertheless it was a pleasure to slap it on. And, as I touched each board, music filled my head. The first board played 'Sunday Will Never Be The Same', a sad-happy summer song by Spanky and Our Gang that you never hear any more. I stroked it up and down. The next board produced 'Kites' by Simon Dupree and the Big Sound. I heard 'The Wind Cries Mary' and 'I Can See For Miles' — 'See Emily Play', 'Waterloo Sunset', 'I Can Hear The Grass Grow'. Wonderful songs. Of course other boards played terrible things like 'Silence is Golden' and 'The Green, Green Grass of Home'. They were painted less thoroughly. But even those schlock items seemed, if only faintly, to have the trace of redemption that I found in every piece of music that I heard at that time.

I had always understood that for me music was an escape route, a way out of the everyday, where I was a mere bystander. I accused myself of becoming enslaved to music so that I wouldn't have to face reality. Yet, kneeling there on the museum grass, under the alien sun, with featureless darkness all around, it came to me that the music that I loved first, that I had listened to most closely, and knew every word of, wasn't any escape. *There's a crack up in the ceiling, and the kitchen sink is leaking. Nobody feels any pain. What a field day for the heat, a thousand people in the street, singing songs and carrying signs, mostly say, Hurray for our side.*

You say you want a revolution.

What I loved then about the music was that, there in the suburbs, it connected me. At that time in this country there was only one station that played pop music — the ZMs. And so if you were hearing it, everyone was hearing it. As I painted I would hear the Chambers Brothers chant, 'Time Has Come Today!' and think, surely. Surely now the world is going to change.

The world? The world at that time was me, and wherever the music came from. India? There was no music that mattered coming out of India, mate. Or Canada, or Chile, or Czechoslovakia. Those places simply didn't exist. History? History was the history of rock 'n' roll, which was being brilliantly invented while I listened. There on my knees, surrounded by bright yellow dandelion heads glowing on the lush green of the lawn, in the sun, painting, and with the radio presenting the new history of the world to me, I was utterly serious — and happy.

When I arrived at the next case and looked down into it,

again there were eyepieces. Peering through the lenses, I saw what looked like a bunch of amoeba. No little theatre this time — this was more like looking down a microscope. No more music (I still had 'Don't Let Me Be Misunderstood' ringing in my ears.) Down there were red amoeba, and white ones, and they were kind of shuffling round, busy, like they'd been heated up. So? I stared at them and I wasn't getting any messages. Was this the primal life of our planet or something? Then, down in the left-hand corner, some letters began to flash like they do on the TV news when there's some new news: LIVE. LIVE. LIVE. So these amoeba were alive — was that it? I tried to show an interest. The red amoeba were rounding up the white ones, kind of herding them. They would bump them, jostle them — the white ones were trying to get away. Every now and then a white one would slip through the cordon, and drift off on what seemed to be a current that was running through in the background. So what was this about? LIVE LIVE LIVE had come back on — so was this like a positive message? Not live so much as live, as in live and let live — was that it?

Then an idea began to form in my head.

That this was about me.

That it was the cancer cells inside me, and the other cells, what did the oncologist call them? the defender cells, maybe — the red ones, were trying to fight those horrible white ones, which, now that I studied them, seemed to be like holes with no content, nothing of me in them. And my guys, the red ones, they were working away like anything, I could see that now, in heroic fashion, trying to get those white ones. Hey, guys, hey — get that one up the top there! He's getting away!

As I stared down into those lenses my fingers came up

and touched the skin just inside my right collarbone. There was a faint ridge, a pale scar. Two years earlier I had found a small swelling there. A lump, in the shower. They stuck a needle in it; it was malignant, they said. A secondary site. Your cancer, they said. They couldn't find the primary.

Being told I had cancer had an effect on me. The doctor said, '. . . your cancer . . .' Those two words were in a sentence he said. Until then it had always been, '. . . your lump . . .', and then this sentence went past me with those words in it and I had to drag them back and examine them minutely. 'Your cancer' — right? Right. The immediate effect was that my palms got sweaty. We were standing in a corridor up on the ninth floor of the Wellington hospital, a tea trolley going past, there was livid green lino on the floor — suddenly I was noticing everything. I felt a film of really liquid sweat appear on the skin of my palms. Sweaty palms is a cliché, but I'd never actually felt it before. It's always good to have a new sensation — I noticed what it felt like. But there was a bigger effect. It formed slowly, like an idea.

It took a bit of time to arrive. In fact, I'm not entirely sure that it has stopped arriving. It's very simple, but it's had a huge effect on me. It's that you are not alive until you know you are going to die.

Now there's a cliché. But it's a cliché because it's true. And for someone like me, who'd so determinedly put the fact of death right out of his mind, it was a revelation.

There was a shock period at first. I was driving home after the doctor said those two words and, going into a roundabout, missed seeing a car that was coming round fast and nearly got sideswiped. I pulled over and spoke sternly to myself: Just because you've got cancer doesn't mean you can give up keeping yourself alive! You can still die in a car crash, okay? Then there was the patch when I felt super-good. Man, I played so much tennis. I got up really early and walked down for the paper. Everyone said to me, Gee, you look really good! That was such a loaded statement. Meanwhile I was rushing round, trying to prove something, and inside there's this huge question mark. It's like I was trying to push it to see what would happen. If I could stand it. And I could. Whew.

Then after a couple of months I settled down. I'd told everyone who needed to know, and I'd survived the sympathy, and I'd survived my own scrutiny, and I'd survived the radiotherapy, and so here I was. Every day I asked myself — Do you feel tired? I was rushing round like I was on wheels — of course I was tired! The truth was, I didn't feel any different. The cancer wasn't having any effect on me.

But I was going to die.

I watched the red amoeba battling the white ones. I wanted to get my hands in there, I wanted to help. But I already knew about this. I had to accept the odd white cell. They were in me. I was fighting them. That was one of the amazing things I learned from the oncologist. The doctors couldn't find a primary site for my cancer. They said it was a melanoma, which they figured out by slicing up the lump they took out of me and growing cultures on it for a month. But they couldn't find where the lump started. I had X-rays, a CAT scan, cameras up me and down me, and every kind of horrible test you can imagine. Nothing. I used to look down at my body in the shower and think, Where? The oncologist said, There's three possible scenarios. Either your primary is so small we can't see it on the scan. Or it spontaneously regressed. Or your immune system fought the cancer cells and destroyed them. Those are the only three possibilities known to science.

I liked that third scenario best. I liked being a fearless cancer fighter. After that, everything I did was to fight off death. That was the new idea I had — that death was something you had to fight, every minute of the day. You could never rest.

Shelley said it made me a bit hard to live with.

It made me buy the pool hall.

It made me a victim of impulse — I would get an idea, and act on it, like I was dying a bit if I didn't. I see that now. But I can't stop. I've got to keep pushing forward. Sure, I'm stuck here, writing this. But that's just something I'm going through. There's something up ahead for me, I know there is. I have to find my way there.

I stared down the eyepieces in the museum of the aliens and I stared and stared. How I loved those red bubbles. They were really beautiful — they had patterns within them, braided traces, like rivers, which looped and surged, and which bound some living impulse — was that it? — each red bubble had an impulse within it. Whereas the white ones were just empty, just spaces in the universe, where formlessness came through. How could the whites resist the energy and complex vitality of the reds? Go, red team!

I just had to watch my death happening.

I stared until my eyes hurt. The longer I looked at those red bubbles the more fascinating they became. They were full of memory and optimism — each one had part of my life in it. That was it. Each bubble contained one of my days. There they were, day after day, teeming with detail, living packages, like potential that I had fulfilled — those extraordinary red bubbles. But still the white ones appeared.

It was a kind of agony to watch. I couldn't tear myself away — if I didn't watch, something might go wrong. Finally the bubbles began to blur. They danced. They rained before my eyes. They were like snow on some inner TV.

My eyes were just hurting too much and I had to lift my head away.

Then I saw that snow was dancing all around me. Snow was running across a screen, patterns of snow, lines of it, on the screen of the TV in the hired room high inside the Hotel Raffaele.

13

After that, I never felt alone.

I didn't like the thought that the aliens had listened in on and recorded my worst self. I mean, I'm for the truth and all, but I'd rather know when I'm telling it. And suddenly it was hard to just be myself — I felt like I was famous. I'd catch myself in mid-shot all the time, turning to the camera and explaining, 'See, what happened there was . . .' Unhealthy.

And I desperately wanted to know how things were going with my cancer. The oncologist felt me up (there's no other term for it) once every couple of months and pronounced me okay to carry on, and until I looked down through those lenses I'd been happy to accept that I was in remission and nothing more could be known. But now that I'd seen the cancer LIVE I had a vision of those white cells all swimming off to form a new lump somewhere. What was I going to tell the oncologist? 'I've had a kind of super-scan, better than your one, and what I saw was . . .' I don't think so. But suddenly I was looking inward again, trying to see in through my skin, and searching for signs.

What did the aliens know? Where my primary site was? Would they tell me? Better — could they influence it? Would they?

Did they know when I was going to die?

Shelley caught me talking to the mirror in the bathroom. I was shaving and had half my face covered with foam. My razor was in my hand, held up like a kind of totem — like someone might hold up a pencil in a meeting to say, I have the floor. I wasn't actually speaking out loud, thank god. But that only made it weirder. About one beat too late I sensed that she was there in the doorway. I caught my face in the mirror, before it rearranged itself. My mouth was open, my eyes were animated and enlarged.

'Don't let me disturb you,' she said.

'I am already deeply disturbed, Shelley.'

'You are already keeping the entire family waiting.'

Having used him as an excuse to stay over at the Hotel Raffaele, I rang Fatty Clark and got him to come in to the pool hall for a game.

I put up the 'Closing Early' sign and cleared the guys out at nine. By the time Fatty arrived I had the place cleaned and under control. All the lights were off except one over the far table and a little light at the desk so you didn't have to pick a CD in the dark. I had two cigars out on top of the counter, and a bottle of Cutty Sark, and Heineken, and nuts, and I had a Tony Joe White CD going that I thought Fatty would like — something smoky and funky and not too subtle. Not that Fatty is unsubtle. But this music was going to be between us, if you see what I mean. Two guys, alone together — you don't want anything too swoony for that.

Fatty, when he turned up, had a hat on. He always had a hat on when he came to play pool with me, but I couldn't help wondering if these were the only times he wore it. It was a spiv's hat, with a little feather in the band. He had a big coat, plain, dark, and he had this coat wrapped around him like he was trying to make sure any of the dirt of the streets didn't get on him. He wasn't fat. He hadn't been fat for years. Fatty and I were kids together in the sticks — in the mid-fifties, in the northern Wairarapa, we attended Rataono School, which had a grand total of twenty-four pupils, and a giant totara tree that was impossible to climb, and cows staring at us in the playground from every side. That is where he was fat, or a bit fat. He had chubby legs and a big tummy and his dad called him Fatty, I think. And Fatty encouraged it. His real name was Randolph. There weren't a lot of other Randolphs at Rataono School.

Fatty took off his coat and threw it over the counter. He made a cat's cradle of his hands and cracked his knuckles. He cast an approving eye over the cigars and liquor. Then he said — he always said this — 'Okay, Fast Eddie, let's shoot some pool.'

In fact, Fatty and I didn't play pool, we played snooker. Fatty was good at snooker. He was a draughtsman, and when he played snooker he seemed to cut the table into rectangles and parallelograms and rhombuses and trapeziums with the lines his balls made as they rolled directly to the pockets. I stood admiring, trying to keep my cigar alight. Suck, suck, cough. Fatty made steady progress around the table, pausing to make a shot, moving on. He didn't like to talk. When there was something to say he stopped and placed the butt end of his cue on the ground and came to attention like a sentry and looked straight at you.

'So how's things at work, Fatty?'

'Dah. Straight lines and crooked architects.'

'You making a bob though?'

'A bob, yeah — but that's about all.'

'Yeah?'

'Yeah.' He tapped the butt of his cue on the ground for emphasis. 'Either they can't pay or they won't pay — and if they can, they can't think, so you've gotta design the shed as well as draw it. It's your shot, Fast Eddie.'

'Okay, fat man.'

And I would take my shot. Playing Fatty always improved my snooker. When you're playing the champ, you play up, you lift your game. I always potted a couple so that it didn't seem like a one-man show.

But my eye wasn't really on the ball. I wanted to have a look at Fatty. This wasn't easy. Fatty was a hider. He kept himself hidden behind his fat name — you called him Fatty and you felt you had him pigeonholed. But, as I said, he's not fat any more. And if you tried to talk to him, he came to attention and concentrated on giving you the runaround. He was always entertaining — he was careful about that. People will let you get away with anything as long as you're not boring. He entertained with his contempt — for example, every building he ever worked on was a shed. He said he lived in a shed. Sometimes he said, a bike shed. Every woman he'd ever been seen with was a bike. 'Oh, I've got this new bike parked up in Kelburn,' he'd say. Makes him sound terrible. But Fatty isn't terrible. Women like him. Is it that he doesn't really seem to want anything from them?

I'd always enjoyed a night out with Fatty. We'd been playing pool on and off for years. Afterwards, I came home feeling as though I was a complicator, that life was simple and that from now on I was going to remember that. Of course, this had generally worn off by the time I woke next morning.

But on this occasion I was looking for reassurance. I think that's it. The recent encounters with the aliens had shaken me. Fatty was a direct line back to my roots, to my boyhood, to the time before, when my condition had not been of such concern to me.

I have to admit it, at this point in my life the world was looking pretty strange. The old everyday world, where we all live, where the new day arrives every morning, and we just get up and climb into it — I couldn't find it. The everyday world is a very strange place, but we're used to it. When you spend too long standing back and looking at it — well, it's not a good idea.

Fatty tossed back a handful of peanuts, then worked the chalk onto the tip of his cue. 'You making a quid?' he asked. We were mates from the pre-decimal currency days. We talked the way a lot of guys talk, in blocks. Fatty would put a block of conversation in place and my job was to put up the right block in response. If I got it wrong Fatty would give me a look that said I'd left the back door open. That I was not repelling boarders. It was a test. It kept you nicely on your toes. But it wasn't nasty. With Fatty you got compassion. You got underlying sympathy. Not that sympathy was what you wanted, of course.

Now Fatty was racking up the score. 'That's four to one, Fast Eddie. You're gonna owe me big time.' Fatty always said we were playing for money, it was part of our game — that we were men of the world, risk-takers. He always maintained that he kept a book and that I owed him $47,000.

'So, Mister Grout, how's every little thing with you?' Standing by the rack, he had his cue held upright, as though it was a spear, and his feet in the good brown shoes were set like the hands of a clock at ten to two. He was rocking back and forth, just slightly. His head was back, the better for him to examine me.

'Ah, Fatty,' I said, 'I'm in the middle of my life, you know.' And I gave him my best shot at a solid grin. 'I'm just rolling through, Fatty. Rolling through.'

But Fatty's gaze had a kind of intensity. 'How's your cancer, Mister Grout?'

'Well, no one seems to know, Fatty. I had the lump cut out, I had the radiotherapy — now I've just gotta hang in and see if another lump gets going.' Inside my body I could see those whites escaping my red guards, I could sense the battle inside me. It was humiliating to admit this bodily weakness in front of Fatty. But at the same time I had it to hide behind. Cancer was legit. It was an explanation for my condition — for all and every condition I might have — so that I didn't have to admit to the aliens.

Fatty's eyes were going over my face like he was searching a hillside for a prison escaper. I could feel his intelligence working on me. Don't we humans know so much about each other. Don't we read the human book. It's our primary field of expertise — what state the humans around us are in. We learn it up since we're babies. We read eyes, and skin tone, and smell, and bearing — this is what we know most about. And yet it's the least scientifically studied. Show me the text books on facial expression. I guess you have to go to the works of the great painters. The old Mona Lisa, just a cliché, but every time you see that face you have a damned good look at it. The best movies. And the text books on what we are? It's all mumbo-jumbo. If you want any text books on that you've got to listen to music.

How much did the aliens understand of this?

Fatty's attention was swarming over me. Then he came and he stood close by — the dark solidness of him. We were shoulder to shoulder, looking now at the pool table. Was it my shot? I couldn't remember. Then Fatty put his arm around me and gave me a squeeze. Personal contact — I was shocked.

Standing there, he was digging around inside himself for something. Finally he managed to cough it up. 'The thing is,

Jack,' he said, 'you've got people who give a damn whether you live or die.'

At that he gave a little toss of his head, a jerk, and his body twitched as though these words had shaken him. Then he reached up, adjusted his hat, and bent quickly over the table to line up his next shot.

First among those alleged to give a damn about my continued existence was Shelley.

Since I had been handed the cancer diagnosis, Shelley had given me a lot of rope. My abrupt purchase of the pool hall had rocked her, I knew that, but she'd never spoken a harsh word against it. She'd let me get on with my life. I could see she was counting — that's one against you, Jack. But she is a person of serious capacity, my Shelley. She could wear a lot, soak up a lot, and continue to shine out like a lighthouse. She gave off a glow that I could pick up when I was miles away.

So when there was a rattle in the lock of the pool hall door, Shelley was the last person I expected to see. In she came, wreathed in her breath, which swirled around her in the chill night air, making her look as though she was in a smoking-hot rage. But when she spoke she was entirely civil.

'Ah,' she said, 'here you are then.'

What could we do but nod?

'I see you guys are well into it.' Her smile slid round the room and came to rest on Fatty. 'Hello, Fatty.'

'Hi, Shell. Come down for a game?'

'That's a nice idea.'

While she hung her coat on the cue rack, I poured her a Cutty Sark. I found her a cigar. Shelley didn't drink scotch and I'd never seen her with so much as a cigarette in her hand, but who was I to say that she couldn't be one of the boys. She accepted these offerings gracefully and looked at me, amused, over the top of the glass as she took a sip.

Her cigar she stroked tenderly, lifting it to her nose to get the best of its bouquet. She regarded it, considering. Meanwhile Fatty was moving round in the background. When he caught my eye I saw that he was shrugging himself into his coat. 'There's a bike that's gotta be taken for a spin, Jack,' he said, 'there's a moon that must be howled at. Whoo whoo.' He flapped his elbows, settling the coat. 'Shelley, your loveliness lies upon you like a moon upon the waters.'

Shelley raised her glass, accepting this blarney as no more than her due. It was a pretty scene, Fatty and Shelley like rivals for my affection in the black-and-white shimmer of some silvery old film. And me standing there like a waiter. I hoped the aliens were appreciating the balance of sensibilities here.

Then Fatty was gone.

And what were Shelley and I to do with each other? Pool halls are places where men come together. Women are allowed, sure, but as honorary men. With just me and Shelley in the place, it took on a different atmosphere. So would there be a showdown? There was nothing to suggest so, though there was a certain tension. Was she going to turn and head off into the night, leaving me to my boyish enthusiasms? Would we tear off our clothes and enjoy the plush surface of a pool table? I could take charge, utter some bland statement of the 'Let's hit the road' variety, and sweep the moment away. But the way I saw it, this was Shelley's show. She'd arrived, she'd come on in. There was something on her mind. So I stood back and let things happen.

What happened was that we played snooker. It was a fine

thing to be part of, there in the late night quiet of the pool hall, with Ray Charles moaning low in the background, and the tables like dim islands, and the coloured balls rolling slowly across the green. Is it possible to converse by such means, to communicate? We were in agreement, I felt, that it was satisfying when a ball found its true path to the pocket. We held the chalk out to each other, fetched the extension for the down-the-table shots. I was deeply attached to the idea that we were a union, a combination, two parts of a whole. Of course, for the most part this was taken for granted, something understood from a distance. This gave each room to live the life that is essentially solitary.

Brother Ray sang 'Lonely Avenue'.

And from the light fitting the aliens looked down. I hoped they were getting this. First Fatty making it clear that all men are brothers, and that we all are free. Had they picked up on that? In their museum you didn't get weird versions of our planet, like they didn't understand things correctly. There was almost no accent, if you see what I mean, in the way they spoke our language, not too much lost in the translation. But I hadn't seen anything that showed they understood what there is between people. What passes between. And me and Shelley there, not having to say too much. The balls rolling like destiny across the green baize. Ray singing his head off — 'Hallelujah I Love Her So'. That background aroma of the cigars, neither of them alight now, but the perfume lingering, along with the bluish clouds which hung, tumbling, up above the lights. The night around us like a city, stretching for miles. Were they getting this?

Ray sang 'You Are My Sunshine'.

★

The smart thing would have been to have driven home in one car. But then someone would have had to catch a taxi in the morning.

I kissed her on the footpath. There was Fatty's moon, a full moon, set high between the tops of the buildings. I watched her go down the street and made sure she was in her car before I headed for mine. I flung up an arm in salute — a fulsome gesture.

When I got into the Wolseley I wound back the sunroof so that the moon could shine on my head.

A moonlit drive, with the telegraph poles making long shadowed bars which swung as I went past. I hadn't turned the music on but I could still hear Ray's voice, coming to me across the miles. 'Let's Go Get Stoned.' The smart thing would have been to drive home, where she was waiting, warm and wonderful. Instead I took a side road, then another, and eventually I found myself myself parked on the top of the Ohariu Valley hills.

What was I doing there? I could see our house down across the valley. The lights in the kitchen were on. It made me feel so good, to see those lights of home, to know there were people who cared if I lived or died. I wanted to cuddle that feeling to myself, to cradle it and hold it.

I settled back against the worn old leather seat of the Wolseley. I wasn't going to fall asleep, I wasn't even drowsy. I had the sunroof open, the cool night air would keep me awake.

The yellow moon was round above my head.

1 4

How many nights has the moon kept me company? While I've walked home along a dark beach, with the white-lipped surf running up towards my ankles, the old moon was roundly there in the starry sky above me. When I walked Pood's dog. Fishing from the rocks in Ohariu Bay. Standing outside the back door with a cup of tea before I went to bed.

Sitting in the Wolseley on the hilltop, I stared up into that yellow mottled face. I was wide awake — but it definitely *was* a face. High cheekbones, long nose. Eyes which never blinked, which studied you but never commented. It was amazing — *there really was a face!* I'd never seen this so clearly before — the man in the moon. I was wide awake, and the man in the moon was there as plain as he's painted in the kids' books.

Sound asleep now, I rose through the rectangle of the sunroof and began to stream on a beam of light up towards the man in the moon. Somehow I was still in the car — the stately old Wolseley seemed to be streaming with me. I gripped the steering wheel. The moon was ahead of me now, out through the windscreen — the car was tilted upwards and I was driving up through the night. This struck me as dangerous and I wanted to do something to stop it, so I honked the horn. It was incredibly loud. It honked massively there in the night air, everything seemed to recoil from it. But it didn't wake me, and it didn't stop my upward progress. As I got closer to it, the moon was immense, its mottled, pockmarked face filling the whole windscreen, and stretching for miles on either side.

There was a gentle bump and a little flurry of dust. Then everything settled. I was sitting in my Wolseley on the surface of the moon.

A bit of a barren place. Nice yellow light, though.

After a while I got out. There was thick dust on the ground, through which jagged rocks appeared. The air was very fresh — I found I didn't need breathing equipment. This surprised me. The Americans must have lied.

I found I had been holding onto the door of the car and with an act of will I managed to let it go. Nothing happened. Okay. So I put my hand back on it again. It was strange, in that barren place the car was good company.

Eventually I managed to drag myself away. I took a step — and went way further than I had intended. My brain said, no gravity, you can go six times as far up here. But I'd gone miles further than that. One step and I was flying through the air. It was exhilarating, though I was afraid of being parted from the car — I knew that if I lost it I would never get home. Okay, I told myself, you don't need to worry. You can jump six times as high up here — so you'll be able to go way up in the air and see where the car is.

When I looked up I saw the Earth, blue and wonderful, hanging there among the stars.

The moonscape wasn't very interesting. Everywhere I looked it was the same — dust, and small rocks, and bigger rocks, and little depressions and little rises, and everything washed in this pale watery light. There was no reason to go in any particular direction. But I wanted to find something. I couldn't quite figure what. There was something in my mind that I was looking for. I kept looking back to the car, checking.

Then I was going up a gentle rise. It was effortless, bouncing along in big strides that made the ground speed dizzyingly under my feet. Then, from the top I saw ahead of me a great line across the dusty surface which indicated where the dark side of the moon began.

Pink Floyd playing loudly in my head.

I stood on the ridge top, dismayed. It was so dark beyond that line. I had a memory of what the deathly dark had been like inside the aliens' museum — I didn't want to go back there. Nevertheless, I headed down the slope.

The dark line was dead ahead of me now. It was like a natural feature, a landmark in this place with no marks on it — a beach, a line of surf.

Cautiously, I went on in.

Suddenly I was in broad daylight. Earthlight, sunlight. It was mid-afternoon, in Wellington, among people. People, God — this was a crowd! Going down Adelaide Road, shoulder to shoulder, the street was packed. Now I remembered! It was Saturday, I was fourteen years old, with my dad beside me. We'd been to the rugby! We'd been to Athletic Park and seen Wellington play someone — the Springboks, maybe — and we'd won! And now everyone was streaming home. The streets were too crowded for buses or cars and so we'd taken them over. This was about 1965. So many people! I was in the middle of people the way I'd never been before. There was no danger. Some blokes were a bit drunk, but they were only singing and stumbling. I was being jostled from every side, but nothing to complain about. Everyone was so happy — that we'd won! And that we'd taken over the road! Hell, we were wonderful. We were the best.

Then, as suddenly as they had come, the people were gone and I was alone and forcing my way forward through the dark again. Alone on the dark side of the moon.

'Hello?' I said. No reply.

I stood in the dark, wondering why the aliens had picked this to show me.

Looking up, I checked that the stars were still there. Cold comfort. I made myself go on, and, in the middle of the next step, the lights came up, well, that's what it seemed like, and I was in broad daylight again, walking along a beach. Beside me was Shelley. Oh, she looked so young! I recognised her bikini — this was from the mid-seventies and we were in Greece. At the time we were living out of a Ford Escort van in a fishing village called Stomion, south of Mount Olympus, and we'd decided to get away for the day — we were headed away from the popular beach we usually went to and instead were walking off along a great curve of sand that ran away, deserted, to the north. Cicadas were singing like crazy. When we were well clear of the town we spread the blanket and got set up. In both directions the beach stretched, empty — no one for miles! Wine in the shade, togs kicked off. We ran into the sea.

As we were coming back out suddenly we had to run for the blanket and struggle to pull the togs back on to our wet bodies. People were coming. Yes, along the beach we could see a party of Greeks coming towards us. Greeks don't appreciate seeing naked tourists, it disrupts the social order.

This was a family. They had a tape machine which was playing bouzouki music really loudly. There were four kids, and a baby, and both parents, and what looked like two aunts, and a grandmother. The women were all dressed in black — in that heat! They were all arguing, talking, shouting, laughing, in Greek. They came right up to where we were and spread their blanket *right* beside ours, and sat down. They insisted we listen to their music and eat their food and hold their baby and talk to them, even though we didn't have a language in common. In either direction, the beach stretched away, empty, for miles.

They'd come to be near us because they thought we'd like it — because they thought we'd like the company.

Then I was in the dark again.

I was just about to start walking when I realised that I was going to hear something. A sound, a sound was coming. A sound like the arrival of a train — it seemed to rise from within the ground. It seemed to swell from under to enclose me. It was the voice of the moon. The voice rumbled. It said, 'The warmth you find, Jack.'

There on the moon, in my moony state, I recognised this as the voice of the aliens, and I was pleased that they had finally come to be with me.

I stood there, up to my ankles in the cold dust of the moon, thinking about what they'd said. As I did, it began to grow light around me. I gradually lost the exposed feeling and then when I looked up I saw that I was in a room — my bedroom, when I was a boy. That faded old room, with my Cubs certificates on the wall, and my hockey boots, and my little bookshelf with *The Coral Island*, and *The Call of the Wild*, and *Tarzan of the Apes*. The room was tiny, much smaller than I'd remembered, but it was wonderfully cosy. There was the dent in the bed where I'd sat for hours, reading — or just dreaming.

No sooner had I taken the room in than it began to change. It morphed, like an ad on TV, stretching and shifting its shape, until it was another room, in England, where I'd lived when I was in my early twenties. This was just before I met my first wife. I lived there alone — a cold time. There was a chair, where I sat and stared into the glowing bars of an electric heater. Tick, tick, tick, and cars hissing past on the wet road.

Then that room faded and in came an interior of another sort, the inside of a car. It was a Ford Laser I'd once owned, and I was sitting in it. There was a smell of plastic, and of sun-warmed seats. I couldn't see where I was parked. I was inside this metal shape, with windows all around. This metal skin.

That was followed by rooms and rooms and rooms, where I'd been alone. Me and the room — I'd never seen before how a room keeps you company. There's no such thing as a lonely room — there's you, and there's the room.

And then I was outside. The walls fell away and I was treading a long shoreline by the sea. I recognised this — it was at Mataikona, north of Castlepoint in the Wairarapa, where we occasionally borrowed a bach. I was wandering north along a shingle beach, with Stevie — he was about ten. For once he wasn't chattering. And the sea was with us, and the rocks, and the wind, and a long white salt mark like a trace running the length of the dark sand, and the wrack of seaweed, the sea smell, and the accompanying gulls. The way that everything encloses you, and accompanies you — this is what the aliens seemed to be playing up in this scene, and it made me wonder: were they isolates? Did they live miles apart from each other or something? Were there just a few of them?

There in the dust the deep rumbling voice of the aliens came slowly towards me and this time it said, 'We admire your need for company, Jack.'

These words thrilled me. I could sense in them that the aliens were starting to talk about themselves, and I wanted this so badly. My curiosity about them was total. Since they seemed to know everything about me, I presumed that they knew this. The voice went on, and this time the words it said were, 'We don't say *everybody*.' Was this said sadly? Then it said, 'We don't have the word *throng*. We don't say *huggermugger*.'

106

I stood there, listening. The voice faded and, though I waited a long time, it didn't say any more. In an attempt to get things going again, I said, 'We don't say huggermugger either — not that often.'

There was a long pause. Then the voice came back, huge and vibrating, like the voice of a mountain. 'You said the sentence, "We were all huggermugger in there," at 5.16pm on May the 12th, 1989, when you were in conversation with Paul Stanley, Matthew Stanley, and a woman identified only as Jerry.'

'Matthew's wife,' I said. 'Fascinating. Okay, okay — so what did I say at, I dunno, 10am on December 2nd, 1962?'

'You were on your own on that occasion.'

'Oh. Where was I?'

'You were crossing the playground at North Wairarapa Intermediate School.'

'Where was I going?'

'To the stationery store, to get Miss Stafford some chalk.'

It was really weird to hear these personal details delivered in the voice of doom. I said, 'I can remember Miss Stafford. Pigeon-toed. Must have had bad circulation — she used to wear gloves in the classroom.' After a moment I said, 'Lovely big breasts.'

'Yes, you thought about them a lot.'

'Did I? What did I think?'

'You were interested in how they fitted inside her brassiere, and how she would get the brassiere on, and how they would look when the brassiere was coming off, and how —'

'Okay, okay, we get the picture.' It was unnerving to hear this stuff in that giant slow voice that took everything so seriously. The words seemed to fade out towards the stars. The whole universe listening to my sex fantasies — great. But I had the feeling that if I was careful I might get somewhere here — the aliens were responding to my questions. My curiosity about them was like a terrible itch. I tried to remember where we had been headed before Miss Stafford's breasts — oh, I could see them swelling now! — thrust their way into the conversation. But my problem was, I wasn't sure how deeply the aliens could read my thoughts. It seemed they had my whole life on tape. So had they downloaded from my memory, where, if this was true, every moment of my life was stored? Or was it that they watched, and had been watching, for the whole of my life?

If they could watch, then there would have been no need for them to have taken me up to their realm — they could have just watched. But then they wouldn't have known what I was thinking. They wouldn't have known, for example, that I imagined Miss Stafford in front of her bedroom mirror. I certainly didn't tell anyone about that, and when I did anything about it they would only have been able to see what I was doing, not what I was seeing in my mind's eye.

So were they listening in on me now? I had to presume they were. What I knew, they knew. So why did I have to speak? I thought very hard, to see what would happen: 'If you can hear this thought, say, "Bingo."'

Nothing. The silence which ensued grew mould and got old.

I decided to try out my voice again. 'What I'm wondering is,' I said, 'you can see what I'm doing — down there on earth — but that you can't get what I'm thinking. To get that you have to bring me up here — right?'

The air seemed warmer now. I had been cold, standing there in the dark beneath the stars, but, as though there was an electric blanket beneath me, I could feel warmth rising.

For a long time there was no answer. Then I felt the faraway rumble begin deep within the moon, and once again the sound began to come towards me. 'Jack,' the voice said, annoying me — I knew what my name was — 'Jack, we can't answer your questions. We respect your curiosity. But you must answer them for yourself.'

This infuriated me. It made me want to kick my toes in the dust in frustration. But at the same time I could feel that I was having trouble maintaining this rage. From below, the warmth was enveloping me, and, as surely as if it was being injected with a syringe, a huge sense of contentment was seeping through me. My eyelids were heavy, I was going under. I tried to shout, 'I know what you're doing!'

There was no answer.

15

I came to in the bright morning sun, sitting in the Wolseley on the top of a hilltop in Ohariu Valley, my eyes bleary, my skin sweaty inside my clothes, a chill breeze from the south coming in the open sunroof to put an edge on the clear, still morning.

Blink, blink.

I drove slowly home. There was no sign of Shelley or the kids. The house was cold. I took my clothes off and got into bed.

The days which followed weren't a lot of fun. Everyone who lived at our house was civil. The kids took their cue from Shelley and Shelley is nothing if not civilised. She keeps things going. And I made an effort — I hired evening help to run the pool hall two nights a week and on those nights I came home for the evening meal. I tried to stay out of everyone's way. But these are the worst times in a family — when there's nothing obviously wrong, but everything is. When someone is. Everyone registers the mood, but it's not anything that can be talked about.

Those hours when I had gone missing . . .

The line between family life being something you get a kick out of and an endless sequence of blank events is easy to get on the wrong side of. Pass the butter followed by pass the milk, followed by thank you. Followed by reading the paper, followed by bed and that was your day. I seemed to have lost a bone in my body, lost the place where I said my lines and played my part. The family went on with their business around me with great patience. Civil, as I said. Yet what had I done? It wasn't like we could say to ourselves, Dad has had a nervous breakdown and we must all be strong.

The feeling was one of betrayal. Someone had betrayed the family. The dad in the family. Me. Specifically: by being unfaithful. The dad was accused of seeing someone else. Was it true? They all looked at me and wanted to know. And what could I tell them? Because it *was* true. The fact that I wasn't seeing another woman was beside the point. I was being unfaithful to my family and everyone knew it.

Of course, no one actually said anything. And the more I tried to indicate to Shelley that I loved her, the less convincing I became. Flowers, little gifts . . . I was patently trying too hard.

So, for the sake of two unaccounted absences, in tandem with the fact that no one really knew what I did at night (the kids, one by one, all rang me down at the pool hall, late, just to see if I was there), I became an outsider in our home. A stranger who lived there. A house guest.

Of course, I did entertain thoughts of taking them into my confidence. I imagined us around the table during dinner, and into a pause I would say, 'I've got something to tell you.' There would be a pause, a here-we-go, over-the-top-this-time intake of breath, and everyone would sit still, studying whatever was on the end of their forks. And I would say . . .

What? That all through the years you've known me I have been the subject of study by an alien species, and that they've probably had their eyes on you too, since you're associated with me, and recently I have been visiting a kind of laboratory of theirs where we are beginning a truly revelationary sequence of encounters . . . I don't think so.

If only I could get them off my mind. But they were like an alternative life which was living itself out inside me. The

aliens. In a trance I walked down the streets of their cities —
lined with trees? Or with computer screens? What were their
cars like? Their food? Their sex lives?

The aliens were real and they were living in my head, and
I would never rest until I had visited their civilisation. And
nothing could distract me from that. Not even the loss of the
life here on Earth that I had worked all my years to be part of.

And now, from the middle of that unhappy time, here comes
Stevie. He steps right up to the window of my memory and
stands framed there, a musclebound picture of health. Dear
Stevie, my boy boy boy, who as a baby grinned madly at anyone
who came near him. He's grinning now. But look, he's got his
punch with him — it's all coiled up there inside his chest.
When the light in his head comes on, the punch will travel
down his arm to his fist, and from there to my jaw — bang!

Not that any of this could so readily be seen when, early
one evening, he arrived at the pool hall with three other guys
all dressed, like Stevie, in track pants and tees, with towels
round their necks, and hair wet from the shower — but, in
hindsight, it might have been picked up by the discerning
observer. The aliens, for example, they might have read his
body language and general behaviour. But I was only a dad,
proud that in the middle of a difficult time at home his son
had finally appeared at his place of work, accompanied by his
mates from the tennis team. A hopeful dad.

Stevie didn't acknowledge me. That was all right — if
that was the way he wanted to play it I didn't have a problem.
He hung back while one of the other guys, who I knew to be
Jamie Rewana, the number four on their team, did the talking.
Jamie might have recognised me, I don't know. I'd been down
to watch Stevie play a few times, maybe Jamie had seen me

there. If so, he didn't let on. This was a tight little group, with big shoulders and arms carried loose — slightly turned in on itself, like a secret society. Like a pop group. Like a gang. I remembered with an ache how much fun it was to be part of a team like that, especially if your team was leading the league, unbeaten. I gave them the best table and let them get on with it.

But when Hairy John McDonald, one of my regulars, came for change for the Coke machine I just had to point Stevie out to him. And when Davy, who was number three on the team, appeared to ask for a packet of panatellas I produced four Sabrosos, my top brand, and said they were on the house. So where was the lecture on how serious sportsmen didn't smoke? Nowhere, that's where. Davy pocketed the cigars with a lopsided grin and sloped back to the table, his body rolling from side to side as though his shoulder muscles were just a huge weight for him to carry.

I searched through the music for a Stevie-type CD. There wasn't a lot. The music Stevie played at home distressed me. It either sounded like trucks crashing, or it was syrupy to the point that all the colours in the house began to run. Obviously, I had nothing in either category. But I did have the *China Beach* soundtrack and soon the whole joint was jiving to the sound of 'All Along The Watchtower'. Funny how everyone loves the sixties music, even the kids. I'm talkin' 'bout my generation . . .

Away down the hall, Stevie rolled the white ball the length of the table to ease the pink into the corner pocket.

After *China Beach* I came up with something by Cassandra Wilson, mildly funky. I could see a few of the regulars rolling their eyes, but, fuck them, I thought. I caught Jamie Rewana snapping his fingers — good enough for me. And then I went back to Miles, *Kind of Blue*, which is a pool hall cliché, I know, but my guess was that these kids had probably never heard it.

I broke out a Sabroso for myself and held it as though I knew what to do with it.

And so the evening passed. I sat there, happy as a little king, chatting with anyone who came near, reading my Elmore Leonard, grooving anew on the pool hall atmosphere.

And then here they came to pay. Again, Stevie hanging back. Okay, if that's the way you want it, son. Up stepped Davy, the big guy with the wussy slice backhand. 'Cool hall, Daddio,' he said, 'really neat. Really groovy scene.'

'My pleasure.'

'But . . .' he spread his hands, 'what are you offering the youth of today?'

Everyone was just slightly avoiding my eye.

'Today's young people have, ah, heightened sensibilities? They really pick up on the . . . ambience? You know, the smoke here is cool,' his mates broke into a chorus of coughing, 'and . . . okay tables, okay cues. Fine.' Everyone nodding. 'But. Young people today are highly tuned to one particular wavelength.' He paused for effect — glanced at his mates and drew them in a little, then he threw his head back and shouted. 'Dad! The music! It's ugly!'

I came out from behind the counter. I was full of confusion. Inside my head I could hear a voice saying, Just let this pass. But . . . my music . . . everyone loves my music!

In the background some of the guys had stopped playing and were watching. I came fronting up to this Davy. He was taller than I was, young and beefy. I faced him man-to-man. 'Thanks, thanks,' I said. Grinning round. 'Thanks. Okay — message received. So next time, why don't you bring some tapes with you. Okay? Here at the Lounge we can accommodate everyone.' This was a big joke and I grinned round. Stevie was in the back, determinedly studying his shoes.

'Yeah, but,' said Davy. 'We were playing *tonight* — right? So we had to, you know, endure?' Now everyone in the place had stopped playing. Forces were gathering. 'So what we're saying,' Davy went on, eyeballing me, 'is, this experience was inadequate to our needs.' Heavy intimidation coming on to me now. 'Am I making myself clear?'

He pulled himself up so that his chest was a solid wall in front of me. A wall I was grinning into.

Suddenly there was a flurry from the rear and half a dozen of the guys burst through. They grabbed Davy from behind, pinning his arms. The other tennis stars glared around — but they were way outnumbered. Anyway, it was instantly clear that no one actually had the stomach for a punch-up. I took control. 'Thanks, guys. Let him go. You,' this was to Davy, 'I've got no problem with what you're saying. You're welcome here. Okay? And — there's no charge. Okay? For you, tonight — no charge.' I spread my hands. 'And just so there's no inequality, there's no charge for anyone else either. Okay? Tonight is on the house,' I said loudly. 'We don't have a problem here.'

The tension drained. Davy turned and growled at the guys who were holding him, but in fact he wasn't looking for a fight and was secretly relieved, I could see, that everything was settling down.

My heart was banging inside me like an old engine.

Everyone turned away, the energy dissipated. Then I looked up, searching for Stevie. And he was standing right there. My beautiful boy, my son of a gun. He had never come forward, and now he wasn't backing away either. He was still fixated on his shoes. The group broke on either side of him.

No one was watching.

I did see the punch coming. It was so obvious, it was there in his chest like a swollen knot, it was travelling at the speed of thought, which is the fastest speed of all, and the thought reached me long before his fist did. I stood there and took it on the side of the jaw.

That night at the pool hall was the strangest I have ever encountered. The regulars wanted to talk to me. I didn't like it.

For one thing, it was hard talking with a bruised jaw. I said before that I took the punch, but I didn't hold my head there for Stevie's knuckles to make good contact with. I saw the fist coming and I turned my head a little and some of the weight landed on my cheek. Nevertheless — bang! Now my teeth ached as though I'd had major dental work. But that wasn't the worst thing. I didn't like the attention. What I'd always liked about the pool hall was the way that the guys kept their distance. We were in a no-know zone here, where first names were the most information you ever got. You didn't have to be anyone. You didn't get drunk. You didn't have to pay big money. You weren't being unfaithful. But you weren't alone.

Now the guys were looking at me and wanting to know why. I told them Stevie was my son. I said we were going through a difficult time at home.

Here was Hairy John McDonald, big like a landscape feature, and a guy called Frenchie, who was a snooker gun, and Mal, and Andy Stinko (I don't know what his real name was — that's what they called him. He looked like a Croat), and a little guy they called Engine. They all called me Jack — and that was pretty much all we knew. But here they were, shuffling, concerned, uneasy, forming a semicircle around the counter. I'd mutter a few words, get them back to the tables, then a new guy would come in and want to know what was the story, and they'd all gather again. In the end I wrote a sign and stood it on the counter-top: MY BOY HUNG ONE ON ME. WE STILL LOVE EACH OTHER. PLEASE — NO FLOWERS. Which did the trick. I put on ZZ Top's *Eliminator*, a misogynist masterpiece, turned up the volume, and we were back in business. *She's got legs, she knows how to use them*, everyone understood that.

16

At home, things were more complicated. Stevie nursing bruised knuckles, forced to miss an interclub match. Me pouring milk onto my toast so I could suck it rather than chew. The family had a stumble in its tread, a heaviness in its utterances — 'Pass the milk' sounded like 'You've got stinking dirt on you.' By dint of keeping on keeping on we made it through to the weekend, but by lunchtime on Saturday, the Pood just had to ask. Her question was directed at Shelley and it had the style of an enquiry during Parliament's Question Time. 'Mr Speaker, can the Honourable Member opposite please explain . . .'

'So why did Stevie hit Dad?'

Everyone stopped eating. Big girl Lynley said quickly, 'It's a rite of passage.'

'A sort of Freudian thing?' said the Pood.

'The son kills the father and then he —'

'Thank you,' said Shelley. She turned her face towards mine and waited.

I noticed that none of the heat in this matter was being directed at Stevie. It was generally thought, in the unspoken way that these things are agreed upon in families, that Stevie was suffering undeservedly — everyone felt for him having to miss interclub. Stevie, even though he was the hitter, was the innocent party here. Dad, swollen jaw, blackening eye, the hittee, he was not yet sufficiently punished. He had brought whatever had come his way upon himself, and there was more to come too.

The dad was actually feeling a bit grim. He was in pain. He felt guilty. He felt he had been wronged. Yet he felt he'd got what he deserved. Emotions circled the dad like planets.

But what was he going to say?

He opened his mouth and sounds came out. He was looking at Shelley and, way inside, I was looking at him too, at the man called Jack Grout who was fronting for me. I was buried inside him and he was just some bloke who was my spokesman, my puppet. But I didn't seem to be able to do a very good job with him. Maybe it was the problem I had in moving his mouth. I couldn't make him sound fluent. But you'd think that might have been to my advantage — struggling on through a wound often engenders sympathy. But in this case, apparently not. Not if the look on Shelley's face was anything to go by.

With hindsight, it's possible to declare this speech as the turning point in our marriage. It was during the week which followed that Shelley decided she should move out of our house, taking our children with her.

I took it as a good sign that it was she who moved, rather than making me. It suggested that my job was to stay there and keep the home fires burning. That there was a home. That I had to keep it going until such time as its family came back to warm it. Small mercies like this can keep you alive.

She didn't go far — ten houses down the road to a balconied palace belonging to her friend Ally, whose house-sitting arrangements had fallen through. Ally and her new partner were off to Italy, perhaps for good, trying for a foothold in the glamour end of the rag trade — Shelley was just what she needed.

Of course Shelley needn't have taken the kids. Or, maybe, the kids needn't have gone with her. But they chose to. Maybe because it wasn't a very big deal — they left most of their stuff at our place and just came back during the day, when I was at work, to get changes of clothes or that book that suddenly just had to be read again. Pood sometimes came, I could tell, and worked on the computer. Every now and then she left me a note. *Hi Dad. I watered the plants.*

So what was it that the Jack Grout spokesperson said on my behalf that lunchtime? I struggle to remember. I've been over this long story of mine so often that certain bits of it have become like little scenes in a home video, where blurry people come wobbling up to the viewfinder and say their dumb lines — after twenty viewings you know exactly what they're going to say, and you chant along with them. And — I guess this is obvious — the words I've written down here aren't necessarily the exact words that people said on each occasion. But the things I've written are the way I remember them. The way I have them recorded in the version of my life that I run in my head. But are they right? The aliens could tell me. Do they compare my versions and the facts? Good thesis subject — *A Study Comparing Human Personal Narratives and The Real Story, by A N Alien.* But the words of this particular speech, which seems now to have been the fulcrum, are missing. They're underwater, can only be read on the bottom of the pool of my memory for an instant — and then the surface rumples again and I see my own face. I strain to get them back.

I can remember saying, 'I'm not myself lately.' And, 'I do realise that.' Their four faces, two of them — Lynley and Stevie — not looking at me, and two — Shelley and the Poodle — looking hard. Everyone listening. Me listening too, to what I was going to say.

These family scenes.

'What I want to say is that I've never been unfaithful.' Was it those words I said, or was it, 'I've never been untrue?'

120

The words of Leonard Cohen's song 'Bird on the Wire' start to intrude here. *And if I, have been untrue, I hope you know, it was never to you.* Did I really start singing that to them? *Like a drunk in a midnight choir . . . like a knight in an old-fashioned book . . . like a beast with his horn . . .* These images come into my mind and soon I begin to picture myself there at the table, at the centre of the family circle, a drunk, a beast, singing (moaning!) in a moonstruck voice that came like a cry of pain from between my Stevie-punched teeth. Trying to be profound. Trying to tell the truth. Trying to save myself.

I didn't know how far things had gone, that Shelley would actually up and leave. I might have done better.

Did I say, 'I love you all'? I suspect so. Did I say, 'I'm desperate'? My guess is, no. I *was* desperate, but I didn't want them to know that. I didn't want anyone to know. It's funny, that has been my life's work, until now — not letting anyone know. So were the aliens more important to me than my family? No, never. It's just that I believed that if ever I told, I would lose that family. If I told, I would lose everything. That's what I have learned in my life — if you keep it all inside, anything is possible. Maybe you can be in the club.

And now at last I am trying to write my whole story down.

So each night I came home and everything was sitting exactly where I had left it. I can't tell you how it feels to see the glass you drank water from that morning still sitting there, cold, on the stainless steel of the bench, half full, the silvery water in it seeming to have settled somehow into a final form.

At these times the ghost of the family is like a torment. You sit in your daughter's bedroom in the middle of the morning, with your cup of tea, sitting on her bed, looking round at her stuff, and a dangerous brew of emotion begins to bubble. Somehow her certificates from school, pinned to the wall along with cut-outs of this week's pop stars and a newspaper clipping titled *Dolphins tangled in web of death*, and the line-up of her soft toys from her toddler-hood, and the pile of CDs, and the best-loved books — somehow these things come forward, present themselves, shrugging off the ordinariness which once dusted them, and are newly revealed as, wait for it, poignant. Her school scarf, tossed like rubbish in the corner — be still, my beating heart! Suddenly everywhere you look everyday things remind you of the world you have lost, the middle-warm, sloppy-busy, bumping, tousle-headed, stair-thumping hurry-up of family life. You sip your tea and sit and the brew intensifies and slides through your body like poison . . .

And still I had the aliens to manage.

That was the word I came up with, as I sat around and brooded, as I ate pizza and fish 'n' chips and Chinese and Meals-To-You (sure, I can cook, but who wants to cook for one? And then do the dishes) and more pizza — I couldn't get rid of them. They were in my life. I had to manage them.

I couldn't have them in my home. I couldn't have them in my car. I couldn't have them when I was socialising, or at the tennis club — so I would have them at the pool hall.

But even so it was strange, having them hovering overhead while I talked to the pool hall guys. Being conscious of them listening in. For a while there I worked so hard to impress them, I sounded like a sawdust philosopher. I went through a phase where I'd hold forth to the guys: 'Okay, I think you've got a good point there, Jimbo, there's nothing like a dreamer to waste the day away. But you know I read a phrase somewhere

once: in dreams begin responsibilities. Now think about that.'
The hall went downhill quickly. It began to attract a pompous
crowd that gathered round the counter to take me seriously.
But everyone wants to have their say — soon I was attracting
every long-winded bore in town. Finally I noticed this, and
reacted. I slammed Stevie Ray Vaughan's *Love Struck Baby* into
the machine and turned up the juice. I could see the regulars
watching from the distance — sure, it was loud, but at least
you didn't have to put up with all that bullshit talk. Within
three nights I had the place back on the rails.

Whew.

I still had to find a way to manage my sense of being in
permanent contact with the aliens. My next idea was that I
had to deal with them directly, as an equal, rather than letting
them always be looking down on me.

What I came up with was the idea of writing them notes.

It started with me scribbling on a paper serviette. Just idly
— *What part does music play in your lives?* I wrote those words
on a napkin and put it in my pocket. And as I walked around
the pool hall, talking to the guys, watching, keeping things
going, those words were there at my hip, doing their work —
asking their question. Isn't it amazing to write something
down? Words never get tired. They just wait there on the
paper, keeping on keeping on. It's effortless for them, those
written words, there repeating what they have to say, over and
over.

What part does music play? Because in my four visits to
their museum there'd been nothing to hear except their voices.
And anyone who'd listened in on my head must have known
that I always had my ear out for something worth hearing.
Music has been my poetry, the cloud I'm on, the dream I'm
in. I'm not musical, I can't so much as play a triangle. But I

listen out like a big ear. And in their museum, not even a three-chord strum.

The next time I looked at that napkin I was at home and stuffing my trousers into the washing machine — I found it in a pocket. What if this had been Shelley and she'd found it? I went through right then and started a little fire in the fireplace and burned it. I couldn't have the aliens here! I was trying to keep our home ready, ready for the day when Shelley and the kids came back, and there could be no sign of the alien presence, in the house, or in my head when I was there.

But I tied a knot in my mental hanky and when I got to work that night I remembered and there in my head were those words, *What part does music play in your lives?*, which I wrote down again on another napkin.

And the next day I went out and bought a little notebook, a rectangular thing you could hold in your hand, solid, with stiff red cardboard covers. I'd seen people put rubber bands around their notebooks and so I did that too, a wide band like the ones the postie drops near the gate, and that band made it seem like the words were safe in there.

I'd never had a notebook before. It makes you think. You think, Is this good enough to write in there? I got into a habit of roughing out what I was going to say on napkins and then when I had it right I would get the book out and carefully write it down, in nice handwriting. I kept the book in my locked drawer.

So there I am, in the pool hall, late at night, with eight guys bent over the tables in the islanded pool-room light, the plumes from their cigarettes rising in slow coils, and the coloured balls rolling steadily across the green of the baize. Duke Ellington, smooth as smoke, drifting from the speakers. And me behind my counter, my notebook there in the drawer, with a stack of napkins. A faraway look in my eye. Thinking back at the aliens. Words came into my head, went down onto the napkin, then graduated into the book. *What games do you play?* And once the words were set down there I could walk among the tables, and wonder.

Do you have beaches? Have you ever thrown a stick for a dog on a morning when the surf is crashing? Do you have dogs? Do you have the ocean?

What's the coffee like up there?

Where do you think you go when you die?

Then, one night, the thought formed that if I managed it carefully, it might be possible to get the aliens to send words to me.

Again, I was in the pool hall. It was a Tuesday, probably my slowest night. Outside, it was raining — I had the street door closed, but I could hear the rain beating on the tin roof above, and on the wall of the north end. Real rain, heavy, the kind that fills the gutters (*Do you have rain?*), and everyone who came in complained about how foul it was out there, and stood about, shaking their coats, and looking back darkly as though they'd escaped something evil. It made them stay, and the hall filled up. But then the rain passed, and they all took the chance and left. It was too early to close, and there was nothing particular for me to go home to, so I sat at the counter in the empty hall, and listened. I had turned the music off so I could hear the rain, and now I lifted the lid in my head so that it was open to the aliens. I got my notebook out from its drawer and read it through from cover to cover. *What kind of clippings do you have pinned to your walls? Do you have drive-by killings? Have you ever had two perfect poached eggs while the sun comes up on a Saturday morning? Are your men hairier than your women? Is ours the only planet you watch? What makes you weak at the knees? Do you have men and women? Don't you think the music we made in the 1960s is the best? Does your skin grow back if you make a hole in it?* On and on, pages of them. *Do you have sex with your children? Do you eat each other? What's your feeling about Rod Laver — the greatest ever? How many centuries have you been watching us?*

Finally my eye fell on a page that had just one sentence on it. *What do your eyes look like?*

The more I stared at these words, the more they fascinated me. Yes, this was the place to start. I began to get the feeling that I wasn't the only one reading them. In the pool hall, everything was stilled. The cues upright in their racks, the balls clustered in their wooden triangles, the green tables — waiting. I had the sensation that my ears had popped, that they were open to a circle of sound which was expanding, spreading outwards like a ripple. The rain was gone. I could hear everything for miles — in the distance, dogs were barking. The words seemed to scramble. What do your eyes look like? The letters were writhing, they were going to rearrange themselves! Yes, yes. But every time I got a grip on myself and looked carefully at the page, my words were still there, still asking the same old question.

In the distance, a truck changed gear.

I stared at the gaps between the letters. I turned a page and stared at a blank line. I read the sentence backwards. The sense that something was coming to me was overwhelming, but try as I might, I couldn't make those six words read anything new. I nearly wept with frustration. I wasn't giving up, I wasn't, I was just going to break my concentration, and rethink, come back on a new tack. Then when I relaxed I saw something very clearly. It was right in the exact middle of my head, I had to look inwards to see it. It was an alien eye.

17

I used to own a book of weird cartoons called *Never eat anything bigger than your head*, a title which I suddenly remembered. The eye was too big to be inside my skull. It was much bigger than that — there was a pain, a pressure, which I had to fight off if I wanted to see it.

Thoughts filled my mind. For example, that the aliens were too big for me to handle. They were immense, you couldn't stand to have them inside you, it would blow you to pieces.

But I was also filled with an overwhelming sense of awe. The scale of these creatures! What they knew! For the first time I felt humble before them. This is what you get standing below the Egyptian statues — but at least the Egyptians were human. It's not a feeling we get often, that our species isn't all-powerful. How little our Earth suddenly seemed! Our little lives, the way we cling to them as our golf ball sails through space.

Meanwhile the eye itself stood calmly inside my head. Was it a single great eye that served them all? But weren't there huge benefits in having two eyes — parallax and all that? And wasn't the universe binary — men and women, zero and one? Two eyes, surely? But this eye continued to look on, milky, pale green in colour, and made of water. That's what it looked like — there were what appeared to be waves, which moved round its surface, spreading in endless lines, and they made it difficult to see into its interior. But then you would get glimpses — as though your mind had made a leap. There was no pupil. Nothing definite could be seen. But as I stared inwards sometimes I would make out interior movement. Immense swirlings. What I caught was something like those computer-generated pictures of Earth's weather patterns, where each element seems to be part of a system, which is affecting and being affected by every other element. I have always thought of our weather as a vast equation continually working itself out, and that was what this reminded me of — something that could never be still, that was changed at every moment by reactions elsewhere in the system.

With the difference that our weather is on the outside.

There were no pictures in there — I couldn't see what the eye was seeing. And there was no body that it was part of. No head. No eyeball or eyelashes. Just an immense thinking ball of water standing against a black background. There were no cables, if you know what I mean. Our eyes have nerves which are like the wires that carry the messages to our brains. But there was nothing like that. It was impossible not to think of this eye as itself being a brain. It seemed to be thinking. But at the same time this eye seemed as though it was only a part, an element of a bigger whole. The brain was elsewhere. But this was no comfort. The eye had such presence, it made me shrink to think what the brain might be like. For the first time I was anxious about contact with the aliens.

It was unnerving to have that oversized thing inside you.

But I didn't want to look away from it, because I wasn't sure if it would still be there when I looked back. Of all the experiences I'd had with the aliens, this was the most powerful. I suppose that's because everything else I'd experienced up to that point had been presented to me as a mirror of my own world, in terms that were my own. But this was . . . the correct word can only be . . . alien.

Looking back on this moment, I have to describe it as

being like the way I changed when I learned that I had cancer. That day, my palms went sweaty — I knew I was going to die. After that, the thing that was me was different. I could begin to see the shape of my life, what it would look like when it was over. And this, seeing the eye, was the same. My sense of the order of things was changed permanently. There was a scale to the universe, and forces within it, that I had not grasped.

I'm not sure I did grasp that scale, then. But I had a sense of it. There in the pool hall, sitting behind my desk, I had the universe in my head and it was expanding. Before that, even though I knew this wasn't right, in my head the universe had the Earth at its centre, alive and vital, and from there everything spread out, getting further and further apart, and sort of thinner and thinner, until eventually you were so far from the living centre that things just ran out — they were too thin to exist at all. But now space had a new centre, and, travelling our lonely orbit, we were just a detail in the margins, a tiny speck in a sentient universe.

I guess you'd have to say that I was in a trance of sorts. I must have been there for a couple of hours or so, though it seemed longer. Then, gradually, I just couldn't summon the mental resources to keep concentrating inward so resolutely. I had a pain to ward off, a pressure. When I blinked the pressure would disappear, and in that instant I would realise how hard I had been concentrating. When in the next moment the eye came surging back I was rocked by it. Then as time wore on the eye seemed to change in colour — to redden, as though it was filling with blood. But I never thought that this was really the eye. This was just my head hurting. Gradually I began to lose control. Finally I heaved a huge sigh, let go, and opened my eyes. The pool hall came to me in waves, all wrinkled. I held onto the counter to steady myself. When, after a moment, I glanced inside again, the eye was gone, and all I could see of it was what I could remember.

I stayed at the hall for another hour or so, walking among the tables. I touched things. The solidness of the place was reassuring. I was still there. I was a man, a human man living on Planet Earth in the sun's solar system, and the sense of the world I lived in was familiar to me. Family to me. My kind. The Coke machine, the green cloth of the tables, the heavy white cue ball — I felt huge affection for these things. I was grateful to them.

A semi-ecstatic state.

Finally I found myself back at my desk and I went behind it and looked again into the pages of my notebook. *Don't you love the way gas stations look at night?* Now the things I had written there seemed a bit trivial. I closed the book, put the rubber band around it, and stowed it in the bottom drawer where I kept old bills.

That night, alone in my bed, in the house which had been abandoned to me, for the first time I felt that perhaps all my troubles had been worthwhile. I didn't miss Shelley, or the kids — no, that's not right, I did miss them. But at the same time I felt some huge confidence that they had only been removed from me on a temporary basis — that I was in the middle of something much bigger than I had thought, that I had only to keep driving down the middle of the road and eventually I was sure to find my way back home.

I didn't sleep. I fingered the bedding, and listened to the sounds that came to me through the night. I imagined that I could hear the sea. The ceiling above me seemed permeable and I was sure I could see out into the night. My body felt as though it was lifted by waves, floating gently between the sheets.

And inside my head, there were dark cloudy spaces, with nebula that whirled slowly. It gave me the feeling of being dusted with something divine. All this was meant to be. I was learning.

Over the next few days, I can't imagine that I made a great deal of sense to anyone who spoke to me. I seemed to be floating. Words floated out of my mouth, food floated in, smells and sounds seemed to carry me like currents. It was a bit like the sensations I'd had when I'd first smoked marijuana, twenty-odd years before, but seeing the eye was different. The eye was a fact, and would never go away — that's how I felt. Also, there was a community of marijuana smokers, who grinned at each other. After I'd seen the eye I felt utterly special, removed from the lower human order forever. At the dairy on Happy Valley Road I bought my lunchtime pie with coins that seemed to have arrived in my hand after a long journey through our society, on their way to this special moment. The money was leaving me, equally I was holding a warm pie which had come purposefully towards its encounter with me. 'Funny how it all works out,' I said to the Indian dairy man and he nodded sagely.

I didn't need to go down to the sea to eat, I could hear waves wherever I was, so I headed home, streaming down the road, my sense of myself elongated, not fixed in time. I stepped from the car outside our house and travelled on inside, floated happily around the kitchen, gathering utensils and sauce. Then I looked up and there was Pood, standing in front of me.

'Hi, Dad.'

My Poodle, all long dark curls, lovely wide blue eyes in a broad, big-boned face — something gorgeous reduced to everygirl by the clobber of the day, which this week was tight tee with hitched-up breasts and exposed navel, loose jeans, formidable dark footwear. The Pood tries hard to be everygirl. But at sixteen, she already has a face that will determinedly go through life looking for something that's good enough.

'Hi, Dad.'

I tried to say, 'Hi, darling.' I tried to float on through. But suddenly a local gravity was working on me. My feet were anchored and all the easy movement I'd been enjoying caught up with me in that one instant. Right there in our kitchen, in the presence of our daughter, I sagged.

I stood, looking grimly at her.

She came to my rescue, saying, 'Going to givis half your pie?'

We sat at the table in the snug, eating together. There were crumbs that I hadn't cleared away. I didn't need to look around to know that the rest of the house was bound to be a bit dirty.

'Stay there, I'll make a cup of tea,' she said.

I couldn't leave the table. I was filled with a strange kind of shame. It wasn't an emotion I'd been aware of before and I wanted to cry. But I decided to try and face her. When she came back with the cups I looked up into her eyes.

The kids — they pull the love they need out of you. They make it be in you and then they reach in and get what they need.

We sat, father and daughter, across the table. I want to say father and lovely daughter; tender father and lovely, warm daughter; loving, patient, wise father and gorgeous, healthy, serious, lovely-armful-of-warm-girl daughter — but it wasn't like that. This was no tender moment. I felt as though I was on trial. The temptation to act, to give her some sorrow, or warmth, or tenderness, was overwhelming, especially when faced by what was a terrifyingly clear gaze. Sixteen-year-olds, the whole world must be full of promise and horror to them. The kids seem to know everything — and yet they're saying, Don't put it all on me! Donna — it's ridiculous to call her the Pood during this scene — seemed such a mix of confidence and terror. And now she had come to put her judgment on me.

Under her blue gaze I saw the last month or so of my life from a new perspective. I had never rung my family. I hadn't tried to visit. They were just down the road — once I'd seen them all in Shelley's car and we'd honked at each other. None of this had bothered me at the time.

'What've you been doing?' she said.

'Playing my old records.' But this was just a plain lie and we both ignored it. 'Donna, darling, I just seem to be going through something.'

'Yeah, Dad, we know that.'

'Some kind of mid-life thing, maybe.'

'Yeah, okay — so what've you been *doing*?'

'Doing? Nothing. Just . . . going to the pool hall, and coming home. And sleeping, and eating, and going to the pool hall. What've you been doing?'

Donna tilted her head to the side, trying for a new angle. 'Okay, so who've you been talking to?'

'What d'you mean? I mean, no one. No one in particular. Hey, kiddo, listen — d'you guys think I've been seeing someone?'

'Okay. Okay.' Another tilt, another new angle. 'So what's in your head, Dad?'

I couldn't get her away from me. I said, 'I haven't been seeing anyone — got it?'

'Yeah, we know that.' She put a hard eye on me. 'Stevie's mate kept an eye on you at the pool hall for us — nothing happening there. You just sit behind the counter. Lynley and Mum followed you home five nights — nothing happening. I sneaked along the ridge and checked on you in the morning — nothing. You're just doing your day, aren't you. Mum got a bank statement — you're not spending any money. You just eat the pies and the takeaways and all that shit, and you just do all your little jobs, and then you go to bed. What's going on — are you on smack or something?'

They'd been spying on me. Bloody hell. The thing was, I felt I deserved it. I'd been . . . aberrant. But it was intolerable — the aliens over me like an eye in the sky, and my family peering in through every window.

'Okay, not smack, it'd show up in the bank statement, we thought of that — but what, Dad?'

'D'you think it has to be something?'

'You tell us!'

It never occurred to me to tell her, that was out of the question. But I just couldn't think of the right lie. I wasn't used to lying. We ran a pretty honest house, I think. I try to be honest. I've been trying to write this down honestly. Okay, I know I never told anyone about the aliens — but no one ever asked. Now, across the kitchen table, with faded blue-and-white checked tablecloth, which was highlighting the blue in Pood's eyes, with crumbs, with sideways light from the window, I tried to do what I'd always done — keep on keeping on. I took her hand and I said, 'Baby. Donna.' The hand wasn't happy, it was scared it was being dragged into something so I let it go. It didn't go far. It lay on the table, where it could be picked up again if necessary. But I let it go. 'Tell me,' I said, 'd'you think I'm a bad man?'

After a moment she shook her head.

'D'you think I'm doing something to hurt the family?'

'Yep.'

I sat back. Then I said, 'Look, I'm not committing any crime. I'm not cheating on your mother. You've watched me — everything's in order. Yeah, I feel a bit weird — but, hell, you guys have moved out of the house! How do you feel — weird? Right! These are weird times. Why don't we all just forget it, and you guys come home?'

Now it was her turn to sit back. 'D'you want us to?'

'Of course!'

'But you never rang?'

'You guys moved out. You needed some room or something. It's your move.'

'Yeah, but you're in it — no? You've got an opinion. You're just going, I can take it or leave it.'

'That's not true — I can't take it.'

Finally she gave me something that faintly resembled a smile. 'That house bugs me,' she said. 'Balconies everywhere — all you can do is look out, you can't get on with anything!'

And so it came to pass that my family returned.

Of course there were negotiations. Shelley came to see me. That was another trial. But it wasn't as bad — apparently Pood had explained that I was going through something. It's astonishing that this bland little phrase can be an adequate description of an actual circumstance — but apparently. Now you, you might say, what kind of marriage did you have? That one partner can go through something and not tell the other? Maybe not so good, is one answer. But I don't believe it. Our

135

marriage is real. We love each other, Shelley and me. We couldn't always talk. Sometimes I felt if I told her things she wouldn't like me. And I liked the way she had stuff inside her that I couldn't fathom. I didn't try and make her explain. 'Darling, when you're not thinking about anything, what are you thinking about?' It's bullshit. You've got to allow some countryside between. You share so much without being able to put words to it. The warmth of human proximity, it's the strongest force on the planet. I wanted her beside me, and that's where she wanted me. It all unfolds and you get older and start to think you can see the shape of it. But try to remember how it changes. Man, it's practically running away with you down the road. It seems like it goes on and on but it's never the same, you're being carried, and when you pause and take a look at it, you've come miles. Miles.

So it came to pass that they returned, and the house warmed up again. I had a fear deep inside that now that we knew how to separate it might happen again. But I didn't dwell on this. I tried to act normal. They were all still watching me, and on the worst days I had the feeling we were on borrowed time. I tried to make the best of everything, and be pleasant. Try it sometime. Hey, Jack, don't buy too many bunches of flowers. You can be selfish occasionally. Well, a bit selfish. No, why should you be selfish — do the right thing. Oh, for Christ's sake.

So it came to pass, and it settled in, and more of it went past every day. The family dog came and licked my hand — it was nice. But it wasn't the truth, because it took no account of that eye in my head and, in the end, that eye was too big to ignore.

18

The worst times were at the pool hall. All that acting normal at home put the pressure on down there, for me to get my fix of alien-time and get it over with. I would get my notebook out and flick through its pages and stop at odd phrases. *If you don't have faces, what is it about each other that you find beautiful?* But all that I'd written was pre-eye. The eye made my thoughts seem trivial. It was too big to get my head around — I had to put up with it being around my head, if that makes sense. It would surround me. It wasn't the real eye, just my memory of it, my idea of it, but I would close my eyes and feel it engulfing me, and the pool hall, and Wellington, and the whole world, all of us inside this pale green, watery cloud — and then I'd blink and Hairy John would be standing on the other side of the counter, in the middle of a sentence: '. . . just like my kids, all full of themselves, clean out the fridge, dump the washing and run, I've been thinking of putting a lock on, but it seems a bit, you know, hard line . . .'

In some ways my mind wasn't on the job, and it showed. All kinds of music got played. The toilets began to stink. I gave away free games rather than focus properly on doing my sums. Worst, a kind of passion went out of the place. The pool hall had always pleased me. I had always been able to spread my pleasure around, infect everyone with it. Now the charm of the place was gradually replaced by something rougher, a surly, hard-eyed, barely veiled macho intolerance. There was almost another fight — guys squaring off with cues in their hands. I didn't care.

What I wanted was some way of spending more time with the aliens without being discovered to be missing by my family.

The notebook, it seemed, was the key. They'd responded to it once — all I had to do was ask the right question. So I set to work. I went through a pile of paper napkins, scribbling phrases, trying things out. But the answer when it came was simple. Once I got my request right it was only a matter of time.

My next encounter began with a complaint. A guy I recognised but couldn't put a name to dropped an elbow onto my counter, set his jaw in the cup of his hand, and eyeballed me. I gave him a watery smile. 'This music is shit,' he said. I did my best to come back from the otherworld where I'd been trying to gain entrance. Stubbly, shaven-headed, coldly blue-eyed, he looked like a child-raper who was between crimes. 'Okay?' And he came round the end of the counter, invaded my space without hesitation, and began running his eye along the line of my CDs.

'Okay,' I said, wondering vaguely what music it was that'd offended him so deeply. *Led Zep IV* — I had to agree with him. Who'd put that shit on?

A moment later we were listening to Dusty. I hadn't played her since she'd been the voice of the aliens — go, rapist. He blinked his scary blues at me, and went back to the corner table, where I saw he was beating the pants off Hairy John.

The phrase I'd finally deemed precise enough to write in the notebook wasn't poetic in the least. It was a straight demand. *I want you to come here, to the pool hall, during working hours.*

Well, maybe they liked Dusty too. It was hard not to. She sang those classics as though she was making history. I knew all the words. So did everyone else, it seemed — before we were halfway through the CD a new atmosphere had been induced. Things were better, as that old Camp Grenada song says. The balls rolled as though under a spell — every shot seemed to drop.

For the first time in a week I sat up and looked around. On the counter in front of me I had my notebook open, and the words I'd written were lying there, naked on the page, as though I wanted the sky to read them. I felt something go up my spine — a tingle. My scalp began to tingle too. Something was going to happen. The aliens were going to come. They were going to come to my pool hall and everyone who was here was going to see them. We'd ring the TV and the whole nation would see them. It was over! It was going to be over!

When I looked out across the tables I saw an English guy called Terry Denby shoot a ball and I knew that unworldly laws of gravity had started to operate. Terry's ball moved slowly, serenely, across the green and nudged a red into a pocket. It clipped the pink, which dropped. But it didn't lose speed. A bump here, a kiss there — as though it had a motor inside it, Terry's shot was rolling on to clear every ball from the table.

But Terry wasn't disturbed, because it was happening everywhere. Looking around, I saw that all the guys had become masters. Each shot ended the game by clearing the table. The balls rolled as though on oiled wheels. The music soared over it all — *far, far away, to my island of dreams.* Each new game was one stroke long — no one minded. Everyone moved as though these single-stroke games were the norm. They watched the balls, smiling blandly; they moved slowly, entranced. Smoke rose from the ashtrays, the Coke machine glowed, the music slid from the speakers. My spine seemed to have mercury rising in it.

From my position behind the counter I saw now that the walls were missing.

I have to say that I had never looked very hard at the walls of the pool hall. I had painted them, pale yellow, not long after I bought the place, which was a good colour — it took well on the concrete, and it disguised the staining from the smoke. But in a pool hall you don't want people looking at the walls, the walls are just there to attach the cue racks and score boards to — you want attention to be on the green glowing beneath the warm lights. So now it took me a while to realise that the walls were gone. The Coke machine stood, as ever, in its place, but there was nothing behind it. Just the black of night. The scoreboards, the cue racks, the old movie posters seemed to hang against the darkness of the night outside.

I could feel the blood thrumming in my pipes.

Outside, the darkness was blotchy, indeterminate. There were street lights, and neon, and headlights out there, but there was nothing you could see, nothing definite. It wasn't cold — no wind of night came in. I listened, wide-eared. Nothing to hear, either, just the grind of the city. The guys played on, entranced. I held my position. Out on the centre table, where Jimmy Ronk and The Crazy Jap were playing, the balls had lifted themselves free of the table surface and were moving through the air. Neither Jimmy nor The Jap seemed disturbed by this. The balls played above the table like a fountain.

Dusty came to the end of a song and paused before launching into the next impassioned instalment. In that silence I heard something. Feet. I was paying such rapt attention that it was good that I continued breathing. Something was coming — feet in the distance.

Not running, not hurrying. As I listened out into the hall

the roof that were we under seemed to be floating — of course, there were no walls to support it. I inclined my attention upwards. That's where they would come from, surely. But the feet were coming across the surface of the earth. Out there in the shadows, something was gathering.

Then there were faces. Human faces — not aliens. Just ordinary human beings, who had walked up to the perimeter and were now lining the boundary of the hall. It seemed there was something like a membrane that they couldn't come through. They stopped there and peered in as though they were on the other side of thick glass.

As the gaps around the walls filled with faces I saw that lots of them weren't New Zealanders. In fact, as I searched, I couldn't find anyone who looked like a local. There was an Arab face, and a Turk, and a Dane, and what looked like a Brazilian, an Italian, a Russian. Faces and faces, a united nations. Was that a Maori face? Suddenly I knew that this was a gathering of all the people who, like me, had been abducted by the aliens.

I wanted to shout, come in! People! Talk to me! Brothers and sisters! But I knew that they couldn't hear. They couldn't see me. They couldn't see each other. They were all self-obsessed, all searching. A nation of zombies, they stared in through the wall-less walls at that centre table, where Terry's snooker balls were defying gravity.

Out on the floor, the guys played on. But when I studied them I saw they were losing definition — it was as though they were fading. Inside their outlines, smoke drifted. The Coke machine faded. Everything in the hall had faded, except the green table tops, and the balls which were rolling on them. The balls were being played by players we could hardly see. I say we — I had the sense that I was one with the crowd

141

gathered outside. We were the living here. We were the ones this was all for. We had gathered at my place. I was at the centre. This was a feeling which came over me — a heightened sense of my special importance in the alien scheme of things. It was an impression which filled me with immense happiness.

Yes, a happy moment. At each table the balls were making distinct patterns, some in the air, some restricting themselves to two dimensions. Mandalas, fountains, the DNA molecule. Now I saw that the hall had eight tables. Of course I'd always known this, but suddenly the perfect rightness of it was brilliantly apparent to me. Divisible by one, or two, or four — magic! Eight equal parts of a system, like an engine, which was moving on up to a steady hum. A ripple of energy spread out from its centre, a wave which passed through me — it was like a wave of honey. A bubble of delight went up my spine, to burst inside my head — it was an idea. The idea was that I should get up from behind my counter and walk out into the centre of the eight-part system — the effect would be better there.

As I entered the system I felt its field shift to accommodate me. I felt myself pass through one of the players. For a moment he and I merged — I knew every cell of him. I was hit by a jolt of strange knowledge, to feel what it was like to be him. So different! Such a rough taste! Then I had moved on. My hand touched a table. There was no boundary between the table and me. What a slow life the wood had. In that life all the past was present — the factory where the table had been built, the log from which it had been cut, the earth where it had grown.

So nothing is lost.

In the middle of the room was a place that I was destined to stand. The spot sang to me. I centred myself on it. My feet shuffled until I had the spot perfectly. There! I was wonderfully relaxed. Everything was going to be okay. What had I been so worried about? Not that I'd been aware of the worry, but when I felt my frown lift away a lightness came into me that made my bones feel as light as a bird's.

In the pool hall around me, eight sets of snooker balls made delicate patterns. The patterns seemed to be tuning devices. They balanced the world. In the middle of them, where I was standing, it was possible to see everything. In the guys who were playing you could see their homes and their loved ones and their parents and grandparents and the whole of their line — their histories and the ages they had passed through and the shape of their personalities. And you could take all this in — there was no overload. I could see clearly that everything was both a continually breaking now and the head of an endless continuum.

You could see their body systems, and their instincts, and their memories, and their desires, and their destinies.

And at the same time you could see them as part of the human world, and the ecological world, and the evolutionary world, and the food chain, and the world of impressions, and aesthetics, and pleasures, and as part of the world of physical forces, and as producers, and consumers, and as art objects, and players in the sexual game, and as systems that were living, and as systems that were dying.

This was alien vision.

It was strange — I had never realised that Hairy John was gay.

1 9

And then the moment passed and I saw again that I was in the pool hall and that around the walls were faces.

All around me were the faces of those who had been abducted by the aliens, and they were staring at me. They didn't recognise me. They couldn't see what I had seen. I could tell by their expressions, however, that they were seeing something.

They were seeing me. They were staring. Some were crying and some were thrilled. Some looked grim. They were seeing me and I was another species to them.

I was alien to them.

That was it. This realisation gave me a little shock. I was an alien species to the human beings who were lining the walls. *The* alien species. They had all come here, had all been drawn here, to see the people from outer space who had interfered in their lives. Some of them were angry. Some were excited. But they were all fascinated. They thought I was the most astonishing thing they'd ever seen.

Glancing down, I saw that I still had two legs, two feet, each foot still inside the brown Doc Martens I'd been wearing for years. Jack Grout — same old same old. I tried closing my eyes. I sensed that outside the hall this caused a gasp of astonishment. But all I could see, inside my head, was the alien eye, watery, green, and painfully large. It seemed to be monitoring me — it struck me as being a darker green. Sterner. Oppressed, I opened my eyes again. The faces around the walls were watching me intently to see what I would do. Short of a better idea, I waved and smiled. Sensation! They all recoiled, stunned by what they were seeing. Some of them were weeping. One man, a Dane by the look of his blond forelock, sank to his knees and began to pray. But what were they seeing? It was so frustrating — I felt like a performing seal, clap, clap for the crowd.

Desperately I tried to get outside myself, to see what they were seeing. It was like trying to see what was crawling down your back. I soon gave that up and instead tried to join the crowd outside.

It was a wrench to leave that charmed centre spot. It took a real act of will, and I could see that for the watchers outside I was doing something they weren't keen on. Against a field of resistance, I forced myself forward. I passed through two of the pool players, whose ghostly presences still stroked the cues at phantom balls. But these were fleeting sensations, and then I was near the boundary.

I expected the faces to draw back, but they stared past me as though what they were looking at was still doing its tricks in that central focus. So what would I see if I looked back? Nothing. The fountains of balls, sure. But I was still at the centre of my ordinary old self. So I pressed on. I was right up against whatever it was that held the faces from entering the hall. Those faces were directly in front of me — I stared into eyes that were six inches away. They couldn't see me. I put my hand up — there was an invisible barrier. It was flexible — I pressed it with both hands. It felt like cling film — it gave quite readily. I seemed to be pushing my hand right into the stomach of a Greek-looking woman who resolutely remained right there on the other side of the barrier. Inside my head the eye suddenly loomed. I felt a growing pressure. But I pressed on — I wanted to see what everyone else was seeing! It seemed that in the cling film I could see my face. I looked strained. I pressed and pressed. There was a stretching sound, and then something seemed to pop.

Instantly I was home. That fast. Right then. No blink in the middle, no flight time, no dark passage — one moment I was in the pool hall, hearing the pop of the film, the next I was in our bathroom, peering into the mirror above the basin. I had my work clothes on, and my work shoes that I never wore in the house. I was holding the taps. The mirror was a bit fogged — through the fog I was staring at my face as though I was trying to remember something. It was as though I knew there was something there to be learned, if only I could think hard enough. I was in shock. In my hands the taps were solid — I gripped them tightly. Was there something that had passed through my mind, ever so briefly, during that transition from work to home? Could I reach back into the moment and catch it?

As I frowned, I gradually came to the realisation that I wasn't alone. My eyes moved — I searched the reflection in the mirror. Our bathroom . . . the splashy wallpaper, the underwater theme of the shower curtain, the other mirror . . . Everything was still. Following instinct, my head made a small sideways movement. I glanced down, and there, lying full length in the bath, naked in the clear water, still and silent, was a female human being. My wife. Shelley.

I say she was naked but she was wearing her expression, which was intent. Her eyes held mine. Her expression was not a small thing. There was a strong emanation coming off her face like a force of nature. A hillside, perhaps, a solid barrier. She was not afraid. Perhaps a little bit. She didn't try and cover herself, or look for a weapon. Her eyes held mine. After searching my face she spoke. She said, 'You're not Jack.'

As soon as these words were out, I knew they were true.

In one way I was relieved. I didn't feel like Jack. I didn't want Jack to feel like this. But where was he? Would I ever be able to get him back? Also, I was hurt, no, pained, that there was none of the feeling that had meant so much to me ever since I first met Shelley, that none of this feeling was left. Jack-and-Shelley, that had gone too, to wherever Jack had gone.

In my head, a part of me was still groping back for something that seemed to have been lost in that transition moment.

Leaning against the basin for support, I sighed. 'No, I don't think I am either.'

I turned and examined my face in the mirror again. 'But I look like him.' I fingered my stubble. To me, on the inside, it felt like Jack rubbing his stubble. This sensation had always felt exactly like this. Yes. But the thing that was apprehending the sensation, it I wasn't so sure of. 'I just turned up here, did I?'

'Yes.'

'What, I just appeared?'

'Yes.'

'A bit surprising.'

'Yes, it is.' She thought about it. To think, she took her eyes off mine and looked up into her memory. Whatever it was she was remembering wasn't making her happy. Now she was a bit frightened. She looked back at me and between us we silently agreed that what had happened was outside normal experience and therefore worth worrying about.

I said, 'Did I fade in, or was there a pop, or what?'

'I wasn't watching.' Now she was speaking carefully, and I knew she was figuring how to get out of this. She needed a towel — I reached one for her. She took it, carefully, holding it clear of the water. Also, she wasn't putting anything that I had touched on her body. She wanted me to leave. But she didn't want me out of her bathroom, she wanted me right out — she wanted me not to exist at all.

I said, 'Shelley, can I ask you something?'

She was holding the towel between us, like a sort of screen. She didn't like me using her name, in case it too caught the not-Jack contamination.

I said, 'Can you please tell me what I seem like?'

'What do you mean?'

'Do I seem like a human being? Or what?'

I sat on our doorstep in the night, dwelling on what she'd said to me. It was just after midnight. In the glare of the outside light the backyard shapes loomed ominous. Presumably somewhere out there in the night the guys were running the pool hall without me. Or was I still there — some more human variant of me?

Shelley had told me that she'd been lying in the bath with her eyes closed and she'd had the idea to open them — that's what she said — and as she did, well, there I was. Holding the taps. She told me that I seemed like a human being. That I seemed like Jack. But that I wasn't him.

'Okay, who do you think I am?'

'You're a version of him.'

'Like a clone.'

'Yes, but the Jack bit is missing.'

As I pondered this remark she dropped the towel, plucked her robe from the rail, and pulled it around her wet body. Then she looked at me as though she could finally focus on my difficulty. I saw that now she was really starting to give some thought to the fact that I had just appeared. A frown formed on her famously clear brow. One part of me — an unattractive part? — was pleased, that finally someone else was going to have to deal with the unworldly occurrences that had given me such trouble throughout my life. Another part hoped that Shelley and I might be united by this experience we'd shared. But as we gazed at each other I saw with increasing grimness that it wasn't going to be so — that I had embraced experiences of this sort and she was going to reject them. Shelley was so worldly. Right in the middle of those troubled moments I thought that the aliens had chosen the wrong person, that she was so much more solid than me. In the bath she'd looked like a wonderful example of her species — lightly freckled and smooth-skinned and equipped with all the limbs and surfaces and depths that the human is supposed to have. Whereas I . . . I was just some loser sitting on a doorstep under a naked lightbulb.

She'd said I seemed human. She'd said this with a straight face, even though it's a ridiculous thing to say, and so I presumed that by that time she had started to see what the unusual manner of my arrival might mean. She'd said it with compassion. But that didn't mean she was giving an inch. She wanted to end the transaction. She wanted me out.

As I sat there I began to focus on what she might have meant when she said I wasn't Jack. I'd thought she might see the alien for me. But she only saw something that looked exactly like me. So what did she mean, that I was a version of Jack but was missing the Jack bit? Was she admitting some kind of recognition here? Sorry, I know I'm going on about this, but I have to tell you — for the whole of my life I'd carried this knowledge inside me like a secret, and now here was someone, a solid, sane person, who might share the secret with me.

So I was full of hope when the back door opened and

Shelley, dressed now in jeans and a black sweater, stepped out into the light.

'Pood's awake,' she said. This was a warning — don't you be doing anything which might frighten the horses. I nodded to show that I understood.

Our back door opens directly to the outside, there's no porch, just a little eave above the door and a broad grey square of old concrete. Shelley has softened this with a semicircle of plants in ochre-coloured pots, but concrete is concrete. When we sat out, we usually went up the back, to a spot we'd flattened for picnics, but this wasn't that sort of occasion. This was sitting down in the night to get a few things straight. A concrete occasion.

But I wasn't feeling very concrete.

Rather than sit beside me, she upended a large pot and settled herself on that. Her legs were crossed, and her arms were folded across her chest, as though she was closed to me. But when her gaze finally came round to mine it held the look which had been one of the constants of my life — an openness to the facts, a warmth, a curiosity. Then she said 'So what's this all about?'

I took a deep breath. Then I started in on telling her.

It took ages. I skipped lots of details, but I was careful to go back to when I was nine, to the visits to the shrink, to convey that this wasn't some fad, some stage I was going through. She got cold and I went inside and fetched her a blanket — anything to keep her there. Finally someone was listening.

At some point Pood came down and opened the door, sleepy. 'What're you doing?'

'Talking,' I said.

'That's never a good sign,' she said, and went back up.

I kept going.

I sounded crazy, I knew that. But I had this small point of leverage, which was that Shelley herself had had something unworldly happen to her, this very evening.

But when at one point I paused, she spoke. 'Ah, Jack,' she said, 'you've had a tough time.' The way she said this troubled me. It was as though she was talking about something horrible that had happened to a Japanese tourist, about a landslide in Chile which had destroyed many homes. The light over the door burned brightly, attracting moths, which made maddening circles. A great green moth with burning red eyes landed on the concrete and stayed there, crawling in circles, its wings tight along its sides, as though dazed. 'Look, a puriri moth,' I said. 'They're quite rare now.' I'd always been the one in the family who knew this kind of thing, the names of the birds and the beasts, and this temporary return to normality brought a small smile to Shelley's lips. But it faded. Her face in that lightbulb light looked blotchy, yellowed. She had always sat still to listen and now she was listening carefully. But the stillness which gradually overcame her was not a pretty thing. Wrapped in her blanket, she was as distant as the moon in the night.

My narrative, wandering, obsessed, with me always there at its centre, went on and on. Me at the centre of this other world. This other world which was right here, right at hand, for me. Not for her, though — I was in no doubt about that. As I spoke I could feel myself leaving her. I was talking myself into the distance.

Then, without much warning, we were closing in on the present. I was describing the crowd around the walls of the pool hall, earlier in this long, endless night. I described the incredible frustration I felt at not being able to see the aliens when they were so close, and how I pressed into the film-like barrier. Then I was through the film, and into our bathroom. 'I stared into the mirror,' I said, 'and suddenly I recognised it. Our shower curtain. Though I didn't know you were there.'

Then that was that.

I just stopped. I could feel some final statement, some summary forming on my tongue and, for once in my life, I was wise and didn't speak.

But this didn't save me. Shelley made no move. She was so still inside her blanket. The moths whirled. She looked past me, out into the night. The aliens, it seemed to me, were all around us, close, listening. They were part of this. But Shelley didn't seem likely to acknowledge that. She was looking out to where they were but she wasn't seeing them. Finally she said, 'What a story.' She said, 'Hey, Jacky. You inside that life.' From many miles away, her eyes came round to meet mine. 'Whatever — it's true for you, isn't it.' Such extraordinary eyes, full at the same time of warmth and distance. 'You'll have to go, won't you. You have to meet them, that's what this has all been building up to, and there'll be no peace until you have.'

She sighed.

Then she took me by the hand and took me inside and made love to me. Took me by the hand. Led me. You can say we had sex if you want. She made love to me very tenderly, slowly, carefully. This person who was not Jack, she was kind to him. She concentrated on the moment, just us, married for so many years, there in our bed. She didn't seem embarrassed that the aliens were watching. Then she got me up, and dressed, and out of the house.

I walked off down the drive. Our drive slopes steeply and as I went I felt I was falling down it. She was there on the doorstep, watching. I didn't look back.

Something so strong.

20

I didn't feel strong. When I got to the bottom of the drive I had the choice of turning to the left or to the right. Right led down to the sea. I could just see myself, stomping along above the high-water mark, wind in my teeth, shoes struggling for a grip in the sloping sand — no, thanks, and I made myself turn left, up the long slope of Happy Valley Road, towards the city.

Walk, walk, walk. At one point I sat down and sobbed. It was just past the exit to the tip, there were no houses. I don't know how long I was there. Then I got up and kept on walking.

It was near dawn. A pale, muddy light was spreading over the hills, I could see it when I lifted my head and looked up out of the valley and as I walked I watched the light come. I had the coat that Shelley had dressed me in, my best coat, and good shoes — she'd dressed me as though I was going for a job interview. I had my wallet. I took it out and looked inside. There was my Eftpos card, there was my Visa. Inside the zip pocket was forty-six dollars. She must have slipped forty of that in there.

Up the road.

I passed the spot where the aliens had first stopped my car. There were no signs, no burns in the grass, no metallic smell. Even the goat was gone. It was all inside my head.

Up the road and into Brooklyn.

I pictured the pool hall, with the guys still in it, playing the alien game. Shelley would go down and lock it all up. She would take care of the worldlies. None of that was my problem any more. I steadied my gaze on a picture of Shelley's face, on her eyes as I'd looked at them in the night outside our back door, and I kept going.

Over the crest of Brooklyn, down past the Renouf Centre, down into the upper end of Willis Street. Walk, walk. Down Willis and into Lambton Quay.

You may wonder how I knew where I was going, and I don't know how to answer. I don't think I had an idea formed. I didn't have a plan. But I had a direction. Like a bird, I was going north.

On the streets, cars were moving swiftly over the grey tarmac — swarming, it seemed. *Millions of people, swarming like flies round, Waterloo Underground.* People walking quickly, heads down, deep inside themselves. I walked among them, unnoticed. Lying on the dirty surface of the footpath I saw a large petal, from a magnolia maybe. And further on, another. Every fifty metres, another magnolia petal. I followed the petals and quite soon was leaving the shops behind and diving into a tunnel which went under the road. They led to a bearded busker who was standing in a circle of petals to bounce his song off the subway walls. *As long as I gaze on Waterloo sunset, I am in Paradise.* I tossed him a gold coin, which left me forty-four dollars. Then I was standing at the ticket window of Wellington Station and forking more of them over. 'One way to Paekak, please.' A stiff rectangle of card in my hand, I went to sit on the cold platform to await my train.

Through the cold the train came clanking up and slid to a halt. A short sit in the overheated warmth and then we were away, through the back yards and the cuttings and the sudden tunnels. Every now and then the train straightened and I could see right up its spine, right through all the carriages to the driver's window, a distant square of smeared light, that we were rushing towards. I had a sense that there was a window like that in my head. I was following a dirty beam.

Around me, faces came and went as people got on and off. The train jerked, paused, ran on. Then we were sliding to a standstill and, on a lengthy sign, I read the single black word, *Paekakariki*.

Climbing down, I was out in the cold world again. I crossed the tracks and began walking beside the highway. There was no footpath and the speeding cars were uncomfortably close. But I was no longer in charge of my life, I was merely serving an instinct, trying to climb to a window, and I would take whatever came in its pursuit. Somehow, I didn't think that was going to be a car accident.

I had walked the edge of this road a few times as a teenager. Thirty-odd years before, at the beginning of the school holidays, I took that same early train to Paekak on my way to my uncle's farm near Kaitaia (you'd never let your eighteen-year-old do a hitch like that these days). So I knew there was no point in hitching here, where there was no shoulder for friendly drivers to stop. I trudged into the distance.

Further on, where the road leaned into a long left-hand curve, I hung my thumb out into the wind. Dimly I was aware of all those who had trudged here ahead of me, Kerouac, and Hobo Bob Dylan, and thousands of other lonesome travellers with ramblin' on their minds. *This tune was composed*, went an old song in my head, *by Spencer the Rover — as valiant a man as ever left home.* But I didn't try to remember the rest of the words, or try to work up any of that old blue feeling, so deliciously self-pitying. This was a new path I was on.

A chill breeze played round my naked thumb. The cars which passed showed no sign of slowing. They had made an early start on the road to Taupo, Hamilton, and the north, and didn't want any roadside baggage slowing them down. It became chillier, then, out of a clear sky, a thin rain began to fall. I sheltered under an overbridge. Paekak was well behind me now — I'd walked a long way. I always walk when I'm hitching, it makes them think you're not a slacker. I turn when I hear their tyres, and smile, and show them what I look like. I keep my hands out of my pockets.

But none of these strategies made the slightest difference. The sun rose steadily in the sky — after two hours I was still walking. I didn't care. I wasn't in a hurry. The fact was, I didn't know where I was going. I had only a direction, a feeling that I was following. If I lost it, I was really lost. I would be without impulse in the world. I concentrated on holding my mission steady in my chest, and trudged on.

The car which eventually slowed was not going fast to begin with. A woman of seventy or more was at the wheel of a pale yellow Datsun Sunny. It was a battered old car and its driver had a battered old face, which gave me a long, shrewd once-over before the passenger's door was opened. Where was I going? North. Where north? Waiouru. What was in Waiouru? My brother. Her face said that I wasn't doing this right, that I should be showing a kind of eager desire to get to a destination that I could see in my mind's eye, whereas I was just wanting to be moving. Nevertheless, I seemed to get the nod.

There was a great deal of loose paper and other assorted stuff of a miscellaneous nature that had to be transferred from the passenger seat to a plastic bag in the back. This allowed time for a conversation in which I gave my name, and address, and occupation, and place of birth — each question occasioned a pause in the tidying process so she could study my face while I answered. But eventually a place was cleared for me, and I was encouraged to enter the little world which the car contained. My belt was adjusted for me, so that I was clamped to my seat like an astronaut. Then the horizon was scanned at some length for difficulties. When finally no other vehicle could be seen in any direction, the engine was given an anticipatory rev up. Then we were off.

We proceeded directly to the crown of the road and took up a dominant position there. Many cars overtook us but they were all smart guys and we were undaunted. We had no need to hurry, nor wobble, nor to become flustered. However, it was important to remember that if you wanted to talk and drive at the same time you couldn't hurtle along.

And conversation was clearly a priority. Mrs Grindlay (Pearl, but only a smart guy would have called her that) had voted for MMP, but, as she told me, 'Winston put us between a cleft and a hard stick on that one — thank god for Helen.' It was shocking that they were thinking of charging us for water, which was always there like the weather. She declared that if they wanted to put a water meter on her property they'd have to pay a rental on the land on which it stood. Some of the paperwork now in the plastic bag on the back seat apparently related to this matter. Other papers proved that rust could not be called structural unless it threatened the structure now, not at some time in the future, in which case it was illegal to deny the Sunny a WOF, as happened from time to time. During this part of the conversation I became aware that I was in an unwarranted, unregistered, uninsured vehicle which was nevertheless perfectly safe. I trusted that the aliens had their eye on me and were controlling both this car and the conversation and so I concentrated on being a good listener. Wasn't Kim Hill a beaut? Mind you, the weather has become unreliable, it made you feel you couldn't relax. What the country needed was a new product, produce monster wetas for export or something. By the way, we would be stopping in Bulls for a pie, as the best ones in the North Island were sold there, and anyway what was I doing in godforsaken Waiouru?

Me?

It turned out that I was a military historian who was writing a book about the fate of my brother who had died fighting in Vietnam while using a field gun of a type that was stored in the War Museum there in Waiouru while in a feverish condition acquired as a result of stress-relief activities conducted in unsavoury conditions in the company of a bar girl in a small town just outside Hanoi, called Cheewah — okay? This explanation led to an awkwardness concerning the specific parts of the battle of Monte Cassino where *her* brother had died, a battle which, it transpired, was outside my *specific* area of historical expertise. However, this was smoothed over by Mrs Grindlay who said firmly that it was okay, 'Everybody tells lies when they're hitchhiking.' She herself had picked up and carried in this very car Arthur Allan Thomas's twin brother (brothers were a theme), who knew who had really killed the Crewes, among many colourful others. It was a funny old world.

And so we proceeded, along the crown of the highway, unhesitating and northbound. Pearl made me feel cheerful. I knew the aliens would be loving her and I encouraged her to be herself. Regrettably the pie shop in Bulls had closed some years earlier, she should have remembered that, but we had sandwiches round the corner instead, which reduced me to thirty-three dollars, and then gassed up at the last stop for some time, which reduced me to twenty. By now Pearl was ranging swiftly over a wide conversational territory which included the future of Hamilton (dubious), the aesthetics of wind turbines, walnuts as an investment, the way that roadside fenceposts appeared to have faces on them, and the difficulty of finding a good hat. There were moments when I wondered if I should offer to drive so that she might talk without distraction, but there was an implied insult there, as well as the fact that then I would have to choose which direction I was headed, and so I further tightened my safety belt, averted my eyes whenever another vehicle appeared in our part of the world, and rode on. And so we proceeded, ticking off the towns, Hunterville, Mangaweka, Taihape. There was only one subject upon which Mrs G did not provide satisfaction and that was her own purpose in being out on the highway today. I raised the subject twice but only learned more about, respectively, the right way to attract tourists to the unused parts of the country, and the design of spoons — and, by the way, did I have another twenty for petrol?

Which meant that, as I unfolded myself from my seat and stepped onto the roadside in downtown Waiouru, I was left with the impression that Mrs Grindlay spent her days and maybe even her nights cruising the length of State Highway One, searching for an audience, for new conversational subjects, for petrol money, for ways to keep going.

From inside the car she beamed at me. She told me to make sure I dried between my toes. She scanned the horizon, she revved her engine. Then she was heading north, leaving me on the roadside, wrapped in my coat, with only one thought for company: What the hell was I doing in Waiouru?

So that's how I arrived here.

It's a cowboy town. Set in a desert, the countryside around it is high and lonesome. The tussock rolls like tumbleweed. And in this township the nation's bellies and fuel tanks get filled, in preparation for crossing the barren lands which lie in every direction. This isn't a place you'd stop, unless you were army and didn't know any better.

There was an altitude chill, and a wind which carried it headlong down the road. I wrapped my coat more tightly around me. I was outside a gas station, with a view of another gas station, and another beyond that. The reek of petrol was overpowering. Trucks roared. I wanted to get out of there.

But this had been my destination — as much destination as I had had. I shivered. Suddenly I saw myself in a motel room. Yes. Warm, if a little crazy. Blank pastel walls. I saw myself alive in a room — not sleeping. I knew that in this state I mustn't sleep.

Swiftly I crossed the road and entered a cluttered Mags 'n' Fags. Yeah, they had an exercise book somewhere. Yep, three exercise books, and a biro, any old way you choose it, sport. And then I was back outside in the wind. Waiouru wasn't going anywhere but inside my head my thoughts were running like a tap. Suddenly there was instinct in me, a compass needle.

Between the gas stations there were motels, motels in every direction and it seemed perverse to discriminate. Under the circumstances the nearest one, surely, was the right one, and so I strode into the lobby of Roadhogs ('Where the rubber hits the pillow') and waited for the formalities to begin.

My trusty Visa card soon had me installed in unit 16.

Then the head hog withdrew, leaving me in the company of a room. There was a TV with Sky, which I immediately tuned to the golf, then muted. The bed was as wide as a runway. A Genuine La-Z-Boy, a square chair, a wallow of a couch, a formica disk of a table. Down in a corner, a pile of *National Geographics* and *Playboys* — a homely touch. Homely too was the complimentary cold can of Lion Red, which I knocked off as I paced the place. Apart from the shower and toilet, everything was in the one room.

Pastel walls.

Pastel walls and a big bed to die in. I was tempted. Instead I dragged the formica disk to the middle of the room, pulled up the square chair, and sat down. I opened one of the new exercise books at the first page and held my biro ready in my hand. But it took a long time to get started.

2 1

I wrote everything down. Then I went out to see what came next.

To get the whole story down I was in Roadhogs for three days, during which time I didn't sleep. My phone didn't ring. I didn't eat anything. There was nothing *to* eat, and I thought that being hungry would help keep me awake. I didn't want to encounter the aliens until I was ready never to come back. I wanted to leave something to support Shelley when she had to tell the world where I had gone. At night I drank sugared coffee. I drank the juice from the minibar, and the milk, and the ginger ale. When I got stuck I watched the golf. At one point I was interrupted by the hogmeister, who was making sure I hadn't cut my throat. His eyes lit up when he saw the exercise books. 'It's good to have a project,' he said approvingly, and went off to trim his topiary.

There was a watery green moon watching me from the other side of the ceiling. Every now and then I managed to forget about it.

It's strange putting things down in words, you get fussy, then suddenly you've written pages. Things come back, pictures, your head wants to go everywhere at once.

So you've written it all down. Then what to do?

I'd written myself up to date, written myself to this motel room both in my story and in my life. 'Then I went out to see what came next,' I wrote, and put down my pen.

The good thing about writing all this down was that it'd

given me something to do. As I was nearing its end I'd started to worry about what would happen to me when it was all written, but now that I was there I didn't have to worry. I seemed to have cleared my head, and now something new was coming. I could feel it, it'd been coming for years, it was like a mountain, rising towards me. How to get it closer? I paced the room, trying to figure. I wasn't in a great state, unshaven and a bit grungy, despite regular showers — there's only so many times you can turn your underpants. I could stay here as long as I liked — Shelley would, I knew, take care of the Visa for a while at least. But sleep was closing in on me, I could feel it like a death-drug, and yet sleep wasn't the answer. This motel wasn't the answer. But what to do?

Go shopping.

When later in the morning I walked on out of Waiouru I was carrying a grip I'd bought, packed with purchases. It swung by my side as I headed out of town, bunting my calves. I walked on the right hand side of the road, into the oncoming traffic. I kept my thumb in my pocket. After being contained by that pastel room it was strange to be out in the open world. I felt that I stuck out, that I didn't belong. I kept seeing myself in the closing scene of a movie, walking away into the landscape. Lonesome canyon music played in my head, echoey twangs, the credits were going up across my back and soon I'd be gone.

I was all set to escape the world.

But it's always the same, when you don't want fish all you get is fish. Every second northbound car stopped and shouted across the roadway, did I want a lift? I suppose it did look strange, a guy walking out along the Desert Road with his pookie sack. I waved them on.

The Desert Road really gets us going, doesn't it. We love

that strip of tarseal. It carries us through an extreme zone, where the elements can rise up and say, no go — the way is closed. If you live in town, being at the mercy of nature is rare in this country. So is the feeling of being in a hinterland, an interior. But here the earth seemed to rise up and fill the view. I was in the landscape. The red dirt by my feet had swirly patterns traced in it, like strange writing. I looked around — there was no place to live here.

Into these observations the Datsun Sunny arrived, going south, pulling up so that grey-headed Mrs Grindlay could lean out to shout across from the nearside window. 'Get in, I'll turn around and take you there.' I had a struggle to convince her that I wanted to walk — and that I wanted to walk alone.

As Waiouru fell behind, the road began to climb. There wasn't anywhere to walk on the right and so between trucks I crossed over. Now that I was on the correct side for hitching it seemed that *everyone* stopped for me. No one liked the thought of a man walking out into that dry, barren place. Then finally a cop car pulled up.

The cop was young, about twenty-five, clean-shaven and pale. He didn't look like a local. In my mind Waiouru would have a grizzled old pleeceman who ran the territory with the help of the army toughs. No, this guy was just blatting through, getting off on driving his big engine. He was in love with the car. But he was bright-eyed, alert to me. 'Give you a lift,' he said out the window.

'Nah, I'm walking, thanks.'

'Where to?' He turned off his engine the better to study me. 'Turangi?'

'No, I'm just going up a couple of miles — my brother got killed a couple of years ago, I just want to go on up and visit the spot.'

'Oh, yeah.' Studying me. 'How'd he get killed?'

'Head-on.'

'Yeah?'

'Yeah, once a year I come out and spend a minute with him. It's his birthday.'

'Today?'

'Yeah.'

'Fair enough,' he said. 'So what's your name?'

'James Grainger.'

'James Grainger. I'll run you up to the spot if you like.'

'Ah, no, thanks, I like to walk. It's not far now.'

'Fair enough.' Without embarrassment he looked me up and down.

'So — you the local?' I asked.

'Nah, I'm just on my way through.' He started his engine. But my question had troubled him. 'And then what'll you do?'

'Hitch on out.'

'Yeah, where to?'

'Auckland. Birkenhead — my sister-in-law's place. I'm going up to look after her kids while she goes on holiday.'

'Okay,' he said, and gunned away into the road. As he went I could see him watching me in the mirror. I put my head down, kept walking.

When I looked up again, there was the volcano.

It'd been rising slowly on my left, a wall of dirty brown in the clear air, narrowing to an icy top that small clouds blew past. Ruapehu, prone to explode. It was hard not to believe that the ground was rumbling under my feet. As I walked, one foot after the other, up the steep slope of the road, a memory came. We were in the Wolseley, me and Shelley — I was driving. The kids had flown ahead; we were driving up to have the car for our Coromandel holiday. It'd been a cloudless day, we had the windows down and I was playing a new CD by Chris Isaac. Shelley didn't like it and she'd nearly talked me into not liking it too. Then the volcano loomed and stood in the clear air, and we hit a good piece of road, and Chris hit a good song, 'Wicked Game', all at once, and the music seemed to bring each element of the moment together, so that the car was floating past the volcano. I drove slowly. Shelley turned and gave me an okay smile, then went back to staring at the rising dark cone of rock. The cold air and the car and the road and the mountain and the music all one, and us together there — it was one of those moments when everything was connected up right. The song lasted about four minutes, which is a long, long time.

I had a little weep, thinking of Shelley and our house and our kids and my car and my life, all left so far behind now. I also had a weep stored up there for my brother, dead on the road, which now came flooding forth. Of course I'd never had a brother but now I was having to pay for having talked him into existence and then killed him off so readily. The only thing to do was to keep on walking, so that's what I did. Cars kept stopping. I kept waving them on. The volcano kept rising. The sun climbed. It was almost midday — I stopped for a drink. And the instant I was no longer going forward a huge anxiety rose up inside me. Where was I going? What was I doing? When I started walking again, the feeling walked with me, like a mocking shadow. Overhead a skylark sang. It was a sound I'd always loved, it took me back to my rural boyhood. But now it angered me — the way you couldn't be sure where the sound was coming from. I had to put my bag down so as to search the sky. Ah, there he was, standing in the blue, making a dome with his song. I made myself walk forward, under him. Such a little heart, beating so fast.

Not too many miles ahead of me, I knew, there was a place where this headlong road took a dive into the cold of the earth. It twisted and turned back on itself, humped and then went plunging down into the shadows. That wasn't for me — too icy and raw and enclosing. And then, once the road escaped from that, came the long runoff, downslope from the volcanic plateau and on into Turangi. There was nothing for me there. Or beyond, for that matter.

And so I came to it that I was approaching the place where I was going to have to stop.

I crossed over the curve of the roadway again so that I was on the right-hand side and went on walking north. Spread around me, running away to the horizon in every direction, the ground was thick with rushes and tussock. In patches the earth itself showed through, squirrel-red, trickling between the roots of the plants, a running soil that you could find no firm hold in. Through this ran the long black line of the road and then, rising away on the left, Ruapehu.

Now the pylons reared up, glinting metal, each one a Tower of Babel. They fried the air. As I added them to the landscape that I was going to settle in my hair began to stiffen — I could feel a prickling all over my head. Underfoot, the rumble from within the volcano sent a tremble to my knees. I felt I was sticking up out of the landscape like a cactus. A car honked as it passed, a sound that jumped into the scene and then faded to a travelling moan. The trucks sucked great gouts of swirling air after them. Closer, with every step I was getting closer.

Then I saw, up ahead, a sign.

As I walked now every step was simultaneously lighter and heavier. I felt I was pacing my way to the navel of the

Earth. The wind rushed cold air around the inside of my mouth. Why was my mouth open? But my teeth ached. The road drummed. The electricity crackled. The volcano went boom, boom, inside my head.

The sign stood up stiffly against the firm wind which played in that place. Its paint was cracked and peeling. But I was still able to read, in black letters on the background of AA yellow, *Highest point — 3,450 feet*.

I stood reading these words as though they were the greatest poetry until at last a moment came when, glancing up and down the road, there were no cars. Then I ran for it.

I ran away from the volcano, I wanted the road between me and that oppressive mound, and away from the line of pylon wires which ran across the landscape like a fence. I leaped over heads of tussock, over little dirt clearings. I stumbled onto what looked like a dry watercourse and sprinted along it. A clearing in the tussock came up on my left and I plunged for it, and lay full length against the earth, my grip bag flung ahead of me, my heart pounding.

No one could see me. Even though the road was only about thirty metres away, I was hidden from it. I was gone.

Suddenly I was in no great hurry. I had arrived at the place I had divined that morning in my room at Roadhogs. I was at the highest point and there was nowhere else to go. As the sun curved through the afternoon sky I crawled on between the tussock heads, dragging my grip, until the road was half a kilometre away and the sound of the trucks was still a roar but one that could be lived with.

I found another clearing and settled in. When I looked around, this was a little room, with tussock sides, and a dirt floor. Ants lived here with me, I saw them hauling themselves up out of a crack in the red earth. A tawny spider made immense jumps of an inch, five times his length, and then scaled the side of a swaying stalk. Overhead, the skylark rode and fell as though he was on a string. Everything in earshot belonged to him. The dirt was warm. My cheek was against it and through my skin I could feel the hum of the road, and the furring of the electricity, and the deep rumble of the volcano. The earth was alive, and I was lying on it. I shifted my hand so it was under my cheek and rested my head.

When I woke it was with a start. Sweat was pouring round my collar and the back of my hand was wet with slobber. In my alarm I sat up — which meant I was visible from the road. I ducked down again.

I lay back, thinking. I'd been asleep in a strange bed but the aliens hadn't come for me. This was a first — had they lost interest in me? I didn't think so. I could still sense them, higher than the skylark, a big eye watching down. So weren't they going to come for me here? No, that wasn't right either. This was an alien place if ever there was one. They were close, close.

I drank from my water bottle, settled again.

This time when I awoke it was cold. The sun was behind the volcano, which, when I carefully lifted my head, stood up in the skyline like an immense pointed wave, poised to break over the darkening land. In the gloomy shadows I could no longer see the pylons but I was aware of the charge they carried, which came spreading through the air like a frost. Now I saw that the road was steaming as it cooled. I let out a long breath and was startled by the gout of vapour that filled the air, like a white flag. Someone might see that.

I set about preparing for the night. Using my fingers I scraped a hole for my hip and unrolled the sleeping bag over it. The bag was brown, as close to the earth colour as I'd been able to find. Then I spread a mottled groundsheet and drew it around me like a poncho. Already a thick dew was beginning to form. I kept my head down. But as the last of the light faded there was no great risk I would be seen. I ate dried fruit and drank more water.

When dark settled I stood and walked away into the tussock to relieve myself. Not too far — I wasn't certain I could find my way back.

The night swam with stars. Out here there were no other lights of any kind and so the starlight seemed to dust everything. It was strange light to be alone in. It fell on your skin and gave your hand a ghostly sheen. The tussock was like a frozen ocean. Trucks continued to lumber but the spaces between them got longer and longer. I lay back to study the firmament. As usual on these occasions, I was startled by how many stars there were. Great clusters of them, billows, skeins of light. The longer you stared the more you saw. There were colours up there, delicate pinks and deeper blues, and there were pockets that seemed to be further away. So very many of them — it wasn't hard to imagine that one small speck might have life on it.

It hurt my neck, looking at the stars. They seemed to be still at first but after a while you saw that they were turning and it made you giddy. Then a line would cross them, something moving fast. Sputnik.

Low on the left, a shooting star, like a scratch on the back of your eye, that faded.

My head read a thousand books.

Then I noticed that it was getting harder to see. The stars weren't so distinct. It was as though they were going out. Startled, I glanced about and realised that light was rising from the low hills behind me. Dawn. I'd been awake right through the night. Effortless. I was filled with a giddy, childish excitement. I could control this!

I slept during the sunlight hours and watched the stars at night and in this way three days passed.

Those three days were a time of travelling, of thinking and remembering and wondering. In setting down my story, as I have done, I've told you most of what I thought and so I won't repeat it — suffice to say that I thought it all again, and again, and again. I won't pretend that I wasn't a bit nutty. But you've picked that up. There's no shame in it. I was pretty nutty throughout the length of my encounter with the aliens and that dated back to when I was nine years old. I imagine that many of the people that they've encountered are now in asylums. Somehow, that wasn't where I'd ended up — yet. I was there, in the tussock beside the Desert Road, with a sleeping bag and water and dried food.

After three days, however, I began to worry. I had waited patiently for the aliens, had put myself in their way, and they hadn't come. But I had to see them. That was the only way I could go forward.

Come, aliens. Nice aliens. Come to Jack.

I lay drowsing in the sun, trying to figure a way to progress. I could let myself go to sleep at night and in all probability they would come for me. But what would that achieve? Another visit to the museum of Jack Grout? I had to get beyond that. I had to break through that halfway house, that airlock. I had to find a way in.

When the answer came to me, it was so simple, it made me laugh. It took up residence in my head and then I couldn't see past it. I lay among the tussock, thinking, Of course! The answer lay *inside* me.

This happiness was broken by the thock, thock, thock of a helicopter. I came awake too fast — my senses all ran away from me. The helicopter was coming my way. In a moment I had gathered such possessions as I had and drawn them in close to the tussock. I could hear that chopper roving, searching. Not for me, surely? I hadn't done anything wrong. It wasn't illegal to be out here, was it? But that didn't matter — if they found me, they would root me out and send me home.

The sound came and went, back and forth like a sewing machine stitching the land. Maybe some soldier had gone awol, or a prisoner was on the run? I hugged my possessions and tried to sink into the earth. Finally the sound faded. It was such a relief. I lay, clutching my balls. I was *dying* to have a leak. I had just risen to my knees when, suddenly, the sound came surging back. They had foreseen precisely this — that a hunted man would run the minute they left the scene. I'd been within five seconds of discovery.

The sound shook the ground as they made a couple of quick passes. Then it faded back to where it had come from, back to the south. I lay, holding on. I saw now that I did not necessarily have forever out here, that an accident might wreck my plans, a trivial piece of bad luck. Or my water would run out, or some other problem. No, it was time to make a move.

I stashed my gear, hiding it under handfuls of tussock. I had a last drink, but nothing to eat. Food didn't interest me now. As dusk fell I crouched there in my clearing, watching the light fade behind the shape of the volcano. Then, in darkness, I sat up and set about wrenching my limbs into the lotus position.

It was many years since I had sat in this particular manner — my knee joints groaned. But I put that away from me and made myself concentrate on my breath. Into me it flowed, the moist night air, and out again. The dark settled about me, came down like a roof. The stars swung into place. But I wasn't looking up now. What I had to find was inside. Eyelids lowered, breathing reduced to a slow pulse — in and out the world flowed. I counted my breaths. My thoughts wandered, but, as I'd learned in my twenties, doing yoga every day to help myself cope, I neither denied nor pursued them. Hunks of an old book by Richard Hittleman floated into my head, mantra-like — *the breath is the string, the mind is the kite* — and I smiled as they hovered there like the memory of a song from the sixties. But I could not be distracted. I kept counting — sets of ten, counting, counting. Breathing through the night.

It gets you high, if you do it long enough. In my twenties, unable to find my way, I did two sessions a day. Got me through.

Now I worked on going inside myself. I tried to keep my concentration steady, to rise above everything.

And everything else fell away, so that I forgot where I was, or who I was, or that I was. I wasn't nothing. I was reduced to that one impulse, held still — *find them!* — and then when the dawn came and I felt the sun on my back, I called on that impulse to move, to come to life. Inside it, I swam down into the depths of myself, looking, looking. Down into the universe inside me.

I was still in the lotus position, still counting the breaths. But that was just the body of me. The I, the Jack-thing, was swimming, pushing through layers. The single thought was carrying me: the aliens are down in here somewhere and I am going to find them.

22

From underneath me there came a rumble. It felt like the approach of a huge truck. During the night, I'd been dimly aware of trucks passing, and had successfully let them go, like thoughts that I was choosing not to pursue. But this seemed to be coming ever closer. The ground was shaking. I was shaking — I stopped breathing and came out of the count long enough to grip the thigh that my hand was resting on. I was being shaken all right.

I prised my eyes open, stared around.

Nothing.

Morning. The volcanic plateau. The Desert Road. The volcano. Hello, world.

I took up the count again and, once I was back into it, continued to search for the way in. This time the rumble made me shake so hard that I could feel my teeth starting to clack. I could feel my bones shaking within me — and in feeling those bones I felt *pain*. It'd been years since I'd spent more than a minute in the lotus position.

From the pain came words. 'We're waiting for you.'

These words were spoken clearly into my head. They were uninflected, no big drama, they were just said casually, like some bored health professional saying, You can come through now, Mr Grout. We're waiting for you. I recognised the voice, it was Shelley's voice.

Shelley's voice said to me, 'This way.'

From the direction of the volcano . . .

Shelley, Shelley — what are you doing here?

Are you an alien?

174

Again, her voice said, 'This way.'

I scrambled to my feet — and stumbled. My knees were killing me. As soon I as thought about worldly things like my knees the shuddering rumble stopped. But I didn't want it to stop! I stood, steadied myself and, eyelids lowered, began counting again. Which way, Shelley? Then I began to move towards the source of the rumble, which was directly ahead of me.

At this point anyone could have seen me, I was standing up in the middle of the tussock and not bothering to hide the fact. I marched towards the rumble. I looked neither left nor right, and I don't think it occurred to me that I was crossing the road. I wasn't run over, but that was pure luck. Did a horn wail close behind me? I couldn't say. I had my eyelids lowered and was concentrating on staying on beam.

I guess it was a fair way. As I remember it, there's a good couple of miles of tussock and scrub between the road and the foot of the mountain. But I wasn't aware of any of that. I concentrated on the rumble, which was coming from the volcano ahead of me. Through my eyelids I could sense the lava, red and alive, deep at the heart of whatever it was that lay ahead.

How big can a rumble get? Everything was coming apart. The cells of me were parting. Yes! I knew that I was going to go in between those cells and through there I would find what I was looking for.

Would Shelley be there?

As if the rumble wasn't enough, now something was added to it. A crackling. I suppose this must have been when I was passing underneath the wires which hung from the pylons. But I didn't see the pylons. My skin was alive, every hair on my body was standing — I formed the impression that my clothes were going to catch fire, and so I took them all off. I understood that it was possible for me to feel afraid at this point, but I couldn't afford to take any notice of that. I just kept going.

I came up to the foot of the volcano and, instead of climbing, I just went straight on in.

This is hard to describe, especially since I'm not sure what you would have seen if you been watching me from, say, up on a pylon. For me, inside the rumble, the side of the volcano rose but as I went forward I didn't go up. I went forward and in. Into the ground. I could feel my feet inside the dirt, and then my legs. It wasn't easy going. I had to force my way a bit.

My groin entered the ground and then my waist. The ground didn't part to let me in. As each bit of me entered the ground, made me one with it, I could sense the composition of the earth, volcanic, acid — it rather burned my skin. But that was just my skin. I was also made of earth, I contained earth. And I had to go all the way — I made myself go deeper. It wasn't pleasant, it was abrasive, as though I was forcing a rough passage, and then I began to feel the heat. Ahead of me, in the core, it was incredibly hot and I was going to have to withstand that, because if I wanted to see them I was going to have to go even deeper. The earth was shuddering — the cells of everything were parted and it was that which allowed me entry. My hands went forward and gripped and pulled me on in. My chest. My neck. Then I realised that my nose and mouth would have to go under. Surely not? But I forced myself.

There was earth in my mouth and in my lungs and I couldn't breathe. I had left the world and I was somewhere else. On the alien planet? Nowhere nice, I can tell you. I was drowning in dirt. Earth was up my nose and in my eyes and my ears and I was feeling disgusting. I was dying. This was an absolutely strong, clear sensation — you are going to die here. You can't live on this planet. In this alien.

Into the panic which was rising inside me Shelley spoke again. 'You want to see us but you can't. No one has managed to do it, in two thousand years. We don't think it's possible.' Her voice, talking reason to me.

I couldn't answer, my mouth was full of dirt. I felt . . . disgusting! But I wasn't actually dying. The aliens were here and they were ahead of me. It was simple — I had to see them. So I forced myself to go deeper.

When I was nine, that same year the aliens first contacted me, I nearly drowned. In a river in the Wairarapa, I could feel how the water had closed over my head. As I went down for the third time a hand reached in, through the surface of the water, to grasp me firmly by the wrist and draw me out. A woman. I coughed, shook. I didn't thank her. I ran off along the riverbank, in the sunlight. And now I had the impression that this had happened again — that a hand was pulling me backwards. My own hand? Shelley's? My survival instinct in the image of a hand? Who knows, but backwards I went, painfully, abrasively, through the earth, until my head burst out into the air and I could take a breath.

I stayed like that, with my head and chest out, and the rest of my body buried in the earth. It must have looked ridiculous, my torso sticking out of the side of the volcano like a thermometer in a turkey, but who was watching? Only them. Now they spoke to me through the ground, the words rising through me from my feet. In her voice they said, 'We're inside things, Jack. As you have correctly understood, we are inside you. We visit. We love this planet. Everything is so young. We love to feel the vigour, the energy, the way that everything on your Earth just explodes with possibility.' The voice paused. 'This is what you want to hear, isn't it.'

'Yes.'

'You want to hear about us, to have a clear picture of us, something you can look at and go, that's them and this is me.'

'Yes, yes.'

'You want to hear what we sound like — you don't want to hear your own voices.'

'Right!'

'It isn't possible. We're tiny, too small for you to see. You looked through the lenses in our museum and saw the cancer cells — we're smaller than that.'

'There's electron microscopes,' I said. 'Anyway, you can make me see anything.'

'No, we can only make you see what you're capable of seeing. And do you want to see us as little specks — organless, featureless, colourless? That won't satisfy you. You want to see us in terms of yourself. But we aren't like you. We don't go around on our own. We are always in groups, in clusters. Each cluster has millions of us — we're like one of your cities.'

It was impossibly confusing to be spoken to by Shelley. It was enraging. But on the other hand, they were answering some of my questions.

'Okay, so what do you look like when you're a city?'

'No, we're not a city. We're a bit like a city. And the nearest thing to what you can imagine is that we look like a ball — like a round eye.'

The image of the green eye that I had seen down at the pool hall came into my mind. It floated above me, like an immense milky balloon, wobbling, low overhead, blotting out the sun. But now I could see — there were thousands of them in there, millions.

'Our home planet is round and when we gather like this we make a version of it. This is the shape we like —'

'I know, I know!' I burst in. 'Tell me what the people who lined the walls at the pool hall saw! When they saw me, what did they see?'

'They saw the green eye.'

'Ah . . .' For some reason this was wonderful knowledge, and as I secured it away inside my memory we were both happy. This was a moment of true contact between our species and we both really enjoyed it.

'So you live on a round planet,' I said, 'and you're tiny and you gather . . . so what does your planet look like?'

'There's just us.'

'Yeah, okay — but in the background, the environment? Describe the landscape.'

'No, there's nothing else.'

'You're all there is?'

'Once, we think, our planet was something like yours. That's what our stories tell us. It's part of why we're interested in you. But as we learned to go inside things, gradually we became them. We took them into us. Perhaps we were too curious, too hungry? We don't know, this is all lost in our past. We have stories, legends, there are theories. The current orthodoxy is that we gradually absorbed everything, went into everything, until everything was us, and we were everything, until there was nothing else. We were all there was.'

I rested there in that moment, trying to imagine what they'd told me. My lower body was uncomfortable inside the earth, my chest and head cold out in the air. I hoped I was going to remember all this, know all of this, after. It was a sensation I recalled from the first time I had sex — half of me was in it, and half of me wanted to be watching from the ceiling, recording it. I was scared it was going to be taken from me somehow. Erased. I wanted to get away, to write everything down. But I had a definite sense that this was my one chance, that it was now or never.

That was half of what I was thinking. The other half . . . It's hard to say exactly. I guess the other half of me, the bit that looks beyond itself, was forming a picture. It wasn't like a movie or a photograph. It was as though a culture from a foreign land had given me an injection and allowed me to feel what it was like to be them. But 'foreign cultures' are human — birth, death, marriage, love, music, tennis — we all have those. This was different. This species that had swallowed everything, somehow they disgusted me. It was like having a taste of being a virus.

'So — how long do you live?' I asked.

'That's complicated. We seem to live as long as we want to. Some of us seem to have been alive practically forever — seen on your scale, for immense lengths of time. But we do die. What seems to kill us, finally, is when we lose curiosity, or hope, or interest — when we can't be bothered leaping towards things any more. And that's what brought us here. We were beginning to die out. Imagine — if we put this in your terms — a ball of civilisation, the size, say, of your planet Saturn, that is all more or less one being and then parts of it start to die, to rot.'

'Look,' I said, 'can't we imagine this on your terms? Forget about me. I'm not interested in me.'

'Yes, we know that, but there is no other way we can describe to you what we're talking about. You conceive everything in terms of yourself. Especially you, Jack.'

'I'll work on it. Okay, well — couldn't you use some of your words or something? I don't want to hear Shelley. What do *you* sound like?'

'Did you hear that?'

I hadn't heard anything.

'Okay — again.'

'No, absolutely nothing,' I said.

'No. You can't hear us, in our own voices. And if you did there'd be no point. Inside one of your words we have a thousand words. We are all one and so the words stream between us, and change as they go, each individual adding to them, or turning them, changing them somehow, each communication being followed up, sometimes being overtaken by afterthoughts, and merging, washing back and forth like waves.'

'You're kind of watery?'

'A bit, yes. We particularly like the liquids on your planet, it makes us feel wonderful to be in them.'

'So that's what you do — you come down here and be inside things because it makes you feel good? Kind of like a trip to a health farm?'

'We try to restrict our visits. That's why we make museums — we're concerned in case we absorb your planet. We try to be careful. As we said earlier, our civilisation was starting to die. Some of us could not come up with a reason to live any longer. Some of us wanted to research into what you would call the chemical reasons for physical termination. Others of us went looking for something new.'

'You went off in spacecraft.'

'No, there was only us, remember. There was nothing, only a few trace elements, to make a spacecraft from.'

'So there's nothing to eat? What do you survive on?'

'You might say that we are sustained by curiosity. By our desire to take a leap. That leap creates the energy that sustains us.'

'Huh. Okay — so how did you travel?'

'We made a stream of ourselves. A long thin stream, one individual wide, spaced as far apart as we could stand it, holding hands, so to speak, and we stretched out into space.'

I had the picture of an immensely long tentacle, feeling blindly among the scattered points of the universe.

'Yes, not unlike that,' they said.

'So what other life did you find, apart from Earth?'

'We don't answer that question.'

'I'm sorry?'

'That is one of the questions we don't give an answer to.'

'Why not?' I demanded.

Silence.

'That is so patronising!'

'Yes.'

'What else won't you tell us?'

'We don't answer that either.'

Suddenly I was so angry that I thought, really, that I was going to die of it. I could feel something that would explode me gathering force. This disgusting species, that had swallowed their world and was now being mature about how much it took of ours — it was inside me! The shuddering which I had felt earlier began to return, to build, and build, and I had to let go of all other thoughts and concentrate on trying to calm myself. When the moment passed, I was left with a real fear that this encounter might be too much for me.

'Jack, you see the risks,' they said. Shelley said. I thought I could hear tenderness here and I was moved. But was this their feeling, or Shelley's? I didn't care — I was in a vulnerable state, excitable, desperate, and it meant a lot to me that someone seemed to give a damn.

'I'll be more careful,' I said. I took some breaths. I had come out of the contact and now it was strange, really strange to go back in. I couldn't hear them quite so well, they seemed further away, I had to strain. 'So you found us, and you came here, but you decided not to take over?'

'We have decided not to influence things. We just watch. By contacting individuals, like yourself, we are interfering — we realise that. But we feel it's acceptable, in the larger scheme of things. We try to compensate those individuals whose lives we disrupt by giving them a glimpse of us. We realise this isn't a perfect answer.'

'But you could improve things! You could . . . you know . . . remove Saddam Hussein!'

'You're totally certain that, historically, that is without the slightest doubt the right thing to do? Your planet takes such unexpected turns. Also, you must realise — we have limited power to physically influence things.'

'You stopped my car.'

'That took a huge effort, and in fact the actual physical changes were smaller than you realise. Mostly we painted you a picture.'

'So you're just an audience? You won't take any responsibility at all. You're useless.'

'Do you think so?'

'Useless to us.'

Suddenly I seemed to be uncontrollably angry again. I didn't want to be. But I couldn't help thinking: All of this — all for nothing! So they could have a movie to watch! When the world needs salvation! There was an itching on my chest. I looked down and saw an ant climbing on my skin. My finger went out — and as I was in the act of killing it occurred to me that they might be inside it. I lifted my finger. The ant was half dead — it fell, writhing, and tumbled away. I wanted to tear hunks out of myself. I wanted to get away so that I could think. I wanted a pretty planet with an interesting sky, and beautiful inhabitants. Instead I got a kind of disease.

From them there was silence. I said, 'Shelley?'

'Yes, Jack.'

'Who are you?'

There was a pause. Then her voice said, 'It's so sad that you ask that.'

I let this roll through me. Finally I said, 'Aliens, could you please speak to me in someone else's voice.'

I waited. High overhead, from out in the world, I heard a skylark sing.

Eventually a voice started up again from within the volcano. It was faint. 'We are sorry, Jack,' they said, 'if you're disappointed in us.'

This time it was my voice they were using. But . . . Shelley . . . don't leave me!

'No, no,' I said. 'No!'

'And we are sorry, too, if we have damaged your life. We think we are justified. But that is only us. We do understand that for you your life is all you have.'

I was swinging from anger to loss.

'As you have guessed, this is the last time we will contact you. After this you will be able to remember us or forget us as you choose. We want to thank you for the contribution you have made to our survival. We wish you well in the rest of your life. If it pleases you to think so, we will be watching you with interest.'

'Hang on, hang on!' I fought to focus my attention on the green ball which was fading inside my head. Something vital was being withdrawn from me — I could feel part of my essence being siphoned off. 'Hang on!' I tried to think of something that would sustain the connection. 'Will our planet ever get to visit your museums?'

'We make museums of all the species we think might be in danger of becoming extinct.'

'Is that what you think? Is that what you think?'

'Often our anxieties prove unfounded,' they said.

'Well, why don't you do something!'

'You're one of the lucky ones, Jack,' they said.

Then they spoke to me in the voice of the skylark. I couldn't understand. This skylark sound kept coming and coming and in one way it was kind of maddening. Up and down it went, and no matter how I searched the sky I couldn't find that damned bird. And I couldn't understand. Were they speaking in their own language? But I hadn't heard anything when earlier they'd done that. Were they in contact with the bird? With all the birds? I could definitely sense them, inside that oscillating song. On and on, in a kind of mad twittering.

And then I was sitting on the side of the volcano, naked and raw. I was on my own.

The skylark sang all day and every now and then I searched for him. Sometimes he seemed to shut up and I searched frantically. Then he'd start up again, only further away. He'd come back and I'd start to figure out their language. I had pictures in my head — virus pictures, as though they were the cancer cells I'd seen. So were they the cancer inside me? But there were other pictures too. The skylark seemed to be singing pictures of them . . . another green world . . . green skies . . . neon moons . . . delicate, fascinating weather . . . gorgeous people, with huge liquid green eyes . . . who moved with a slow grace . . . who were waving goodbye . . .

Then the skylark got faint, I could hardly hear him.

Later, dusk came, and he went off to wherever skylarks go at night. And so I was sitting there in the dark of the volcanic plateau, naked, and the night was spreading all around me. But that makes it sound as though I understood where I was and what was going on.

I lay down in the dirt. When I next noticed, there were stars.

2 3

Long spaces, like tubes that I had to swim through, like the silvery insides of a thermos, mirrored tunnels that I had to go down. Long spaces with nothing in them. Occasional moments of looking up at the stars and knowing them for what they were. You're going to die of cold, Jack — that thought coming clearly. Was that my own voice or them speaking to me? But I couldn't find them, and I was pained by the loss of them. Long silvery tubes in which I floated, trying to catch the voice of the skylark.

The world was tilting. I was on my feet but not good at walking. I saw lights, blinding, heard a wailing sound. I must have been crossing the highway — there was a squeal that might have been tyres, there was a shout.

When finally I found the sleeping bag the cold was making me shudder. The shuddering was very like the rumble which had drawn me to them earlier, but I didn't get excited. I could feel that they were gone from me. I fumbled my way into the bag and drew the string tight around my neck. The stars were all falling, raining down like burnt-out fireworks. Like bright scratches on my eyes. Like sparks from a welder. There was a burning smell, acrid, as though my brains were short-circuiting. Sounds ridiculous, I know, but that's what I thought. I shut my eyes, but the stars kept falling. There were long spaces.

Then someone was talking to me. I couldn't get him to shut up. I kept shaking him off, but he wouldn't go. My eyes seemed to be looking directly into the sun, which was low overhead. Then he blocked it out. There was a burning halo around his head. He said, 'Come on, come on, come on.'

I noticed that I was walking. I was holding my sleeping bag and he was holding my grip. He was wearing a cop's uniform. We were walking to his cop car. He said, 'Try and keep the bag in front of you, okay, we don't want to frighten the horses.'

I sat in the back seat of his car, the hot vinyl of the seat burning my bare backside. When he spoke to me, I looked at his face in the rear-vision mirror and I recognised him, but I couldn't think where from. TV, maybe? He was driving, I could hear the siren — then that just seemed to be a wailing inside my head. It didn't matter. Everything that mattered was gone from me. Then when he talked to me I remembered his voice, too. He said, 'I looked it up — there never was anyone by the name of Grainger killed on this road. Huh?' I just closed my eyes.

I saw we were coming into a great city high above the desert. There was no siren, we were just driving easy. I recognised all over again that he was a cop, that this was a cop car, that this was Planet Earth, that I was an alien here — and then when I saw the word *Waiouru* written on a road sign I began for the first time in ages to wonder what was going to happen to me. I kept my eyes half shut, and clutched my grip, which was sitting on the sleeping bag beside me.

'You stay here, okay?' We'd stopped, and he was turning around to look at me. I blinked repeatedly, I couldn't face him. He had a good glare at me, shook his head, then went inside.

The human civilisation was inconceivably strange.

From a million miles away I read the words *Waiouru Police Station*. Everything I looked at was burnt, faded, but those words came alive. I stared at them and then I tried to open my door. It was locked. Leaving the sleeping bag but dragging

the grip I clambered over to the front seat, tried the door —
eased myself out. I went down the side of a building, searching,
searching. Wasn't it back here somewhere? I ran, along behind
a building, turned a corner, and there it was. Roadhogs.

The head hog didn't care that I had no clothes, he just
said, 'Good night, was it?' and laughed his greasy laugh. Yes,
my old room was free . . . and the rest is history.

I presume the head hog deflected the cop. He was the right
man for that job. I stayed in the room in the company of the
pastel colours and we ate room service. I sat at the round
formica table and wrote up the remainder of this story in my
exercise books. At night I slept in a strange bed, and slept.
Nothing. Days passed. One day my ears went pop. That was
all, nothing dramatic. Then I went and borrowed some hog
clothes and tested my Visa card in the shops of Waiouru. I
came out looking like a cowboy, all I needed were the spurs.

And then I was on the road again. I was scared of that cop,
and I must say I wasn't keen for Mrs Grindlay. For long patches
I sat in the roadside grass, trying to divine a direction.

For the first few miles I walked, keeping my thumb in my
pocket. It was a regular day. I didn't feel regular, but have I
ever? The dark road divided the burnt-off hills, heading away
in both directions as though it knew where it was going. I
walked beside the ragged roadside fence. Mrs Grindlay was
right, the fenceposts did look as though they had faces. My
grip swung from my hand, it kept banging against my calves.
All I had now were my exercise books and my Visa card.

A skylark sang.

A skylark sang and I knew he was singing to me but I
couldn't understand a word he said. I could remember the

aliens, but they were like something in a film I had seen when drunk. I was burnt and ashy, and I couldn't reach them. I couldn't feel them. Nothing. I strained. Nothing. I sat down in a paddock, with steers coming to look at me, and nodding grasses, and tried to open myself up. Still nothing. All I could get was that skylark.

Which way to go?

I don't know if I will be readmitted to my old life — or if I want to be. Is this what the men felt like, coming home from the war? At least they had honour. Of course I want to be readmitted! But not on probation. Not out of sympathy either, not as something that's been damaged. I don't think I could stand another punch from Stevie — but without the aliens, I feel empty. I don't feel I have enough to offer. Just the words in these exercise books. And that skylark, who keeps talking in a voice no one can understand.

An ordinary bloke, at market value. What I always wanted to be, just myself, bones and a history, just standing there — but is it enough?

I'll get out my thumb. Head south. One look at Shelley's face will tell the whole story.